<u>VAMPIRE DENTIST</u>

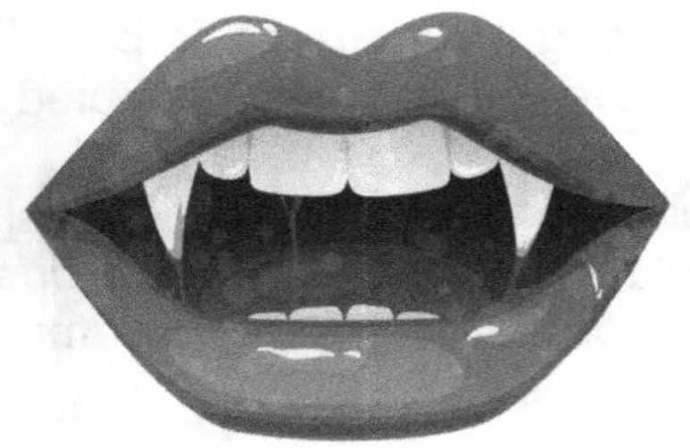

By

Christine J. Whitlock

Adapted from the

popular indie horror-comedy feature film script

Chapter List

Prologue…………………………………………………………..…1

New Venture………………………………………………….6

Looking for a New Partner…………………………….16

New Dental Partnership…………………………….34

The Vam Dent Family……………………………….36

Greenhouse Attacks……………………………….39

Human Patients……………………………………….50

Park Attacks………………………………………….59

Warehouse Attacks……………………………….69

Vampire Patients………………………………….80

About the Author……………………………….115

<u>*PROLOGUE*</u>

Wispy clouds scraped scars against the face of the summer howling full moon. Tall fir and deciduous trees stood sentry in the inner-city park. With her long blonde tresses bouncing behind her, a beautiful young woman strode along a trodden grass path. Dressed in a low-cut red dress revealing her ample bosom, she contemplated what she would do if she were stood up again by that no-good boyfriend. Something glittered up ahead. It was lying between some tall rose bushes in their archway. This was a short cut through the foliage instead of around them. Her high heel stuck in the dewy grass, and she lurched forward and steadied herself. A diamond studded necklace lay sparkling in the rays of the overhead moon.

The young woman bent over to pick up the necklace. That's when the smell hit her. Cold, damp, rotting. And the sound – eerie and unnatural. Before she could fully straighten up, something black, icy, and putrid grabbed her. She screamed and struggled as the dark shrubs enveloped her.

On that balmy same night, a middle-aged woman walked with difficulty, slowly, with her cane along a stone-pebbled path in the large civic park. She regularly strolled here at night. No barking dogs; no birds swooping down for sunflower seeds thrown on the ground; no pesky squirrels begging for peanut handouts. Heard off in the distance was a subtle flapping of wings.

A sparkling emerald necklace lay on the path between high bushes. With her stiff knees, the middle-aged woman with much had difficulty bent over to pick up the necklace.

A black silk-clothed male Vampire jumped out of the tangled foliage and grabbed her around the waist. With no response from the woman, the Vampire with his long blonde hair flowing, tugged, and tugged at her. The woman felt a squeezing at her ample belly, but she only thought it was gas. Bending from her waist, with the hook of her cane, the woman picked up the shimmering necklace.

After more pulling with no response, the frustrated Vampire with his fangs gnashing went back into the bushes. He thought he had superhuman strength as a vampire, but the old woman was a solid rock statue.

Pleased with herself, the woman tucked the necklace into her pocket and continued her walk. Now she was wary of any other glittering objects on the ground in case the jewel thieves had lost more.

Under white full-face full moon as night continued, a burly bearded man in brown corduroy pants and a red lumberjack shirt sauntered along a well-worn footpath in the gardens. A shimmering ruby necklace lay on the dry ground between low lying plants. The husky man bent over to pick up the necklace. Out of the bushes, two voluptuous female Vampires jumped on either side of him, long pointed black nails bared. With no response from the man, the female Vampires tugged and heaved at him, trying to reach his neck with their ivory fangs. The man grabbed the necklace.

As he hoisted himself from a bent-over position, the man at first was terrified at the sight of the two female vampires. After hiding their fangs and smiling sweetly at the man while still hanging onto him, his terror turned to curiosity and hopeful pleasure. Their rotting decay odor was earthy and sensual to him. He entered the flower-covered brambles with one female vampire on each arm. His screams ripped out of the quiet of the night.

That same shadowy evening, two young scantily clad dressed women tugged at the outside door of the inner city park public washroom. The door was locked. "Oh, man, I really have to go," said the shorter of the two.

"Let's try the men's room on the other side," the taller one replied. They ran around the corner of the building and a metal door was open.

Under an exposed dirty lightbulb, the short woman rushed into the cubicle and peed loudly. The other woman took out a red lipstick from her handbag and applied it facing the cloudy mirror.

Pouting her lips, she called out, "Hurry up. The guys are waiting."

The sound of peeing stopped. The sound of nails on the metal cubicle barrier reverberated.

The short tart called out, "There's no toilet paper! Can you get me some?"

A swish sound made the young woman at the mirror turn her head to look. She dropped her lipstick into the sink and screamed. The sink now had a red streak across it. From the back of the men's washroom, a tall figure with a long black cape approached the young woman at the sink. His white pointed fangs stood out from his black shiny skin.

With another swish sound, the short tart in the toilet's banging stopped. Her lifeless body flopped onto the floor with her feet sticking out from the cubicle.

Chapter 1 - NEW VENTURE

One bright sunny day, the back warehouse door in an industrial park creaked opened. Aunty May Lars entered gingerly followed by Dr. Moe Lars, Dr. Pierce Able, and Hans Weiner. They walked up the few inner concrete stairs and stopped at the top. Hans stood in front of the trio who followed him inside: Aunty May Lars – an elderly plump lady with a cane, Dr. Moe Lars – her tall and thin but clean-cut nephew, and Dr. Pierce Able – a long-haired hippy type. Both young men had barely gone through dental college and now were venturing out into their own business.

A bumble of broken chairs, loose wood, and discarded equipment were lumped on the right. Hans walked past them and stood in front of the trio. In his heavy German accent, he grunted, "A great location, yah. Just off the main highway. On the bus routes."

Frumpy Aunty May looked at the makeshift back plywood walls to the left.

Dr. Moe squeaked, "It's a bit more rustic than I expected."

Aunty May commented, "It looks a bit crowded with all this stuff."

Dr. Pierce rubbed his chin. "And the price again?"

Hans stumbled up to him, whispered in his ear, and thumped him on the chest with a big smile. "You can do your own decorating. No extra charge."

Dr. Moe exhaled, "What about all this old office furniture here?"

Dr. Moe gave three sneezes in rapid succession which caused the dust to catapult like Chinese acrobats.

Hans beamed, "Good stuff. No charge."

Hans batted at the large dust particles. "I'll wait outside while you look around."

After the door closed, Aunty May spoke, "After putting you through dental school, Moe, I can only lend you the first month's rent."

Dr. Pierce looked around, "This is really a dump."

The cobwebs and dust sparkled in the sunrays from the top of the wall's north slit windows.

Dr. Moe stood with hands on hips. "If your gambling habit didn't get you such a bad credit rating, we may have gotten something better."

Dr. Pierce poked his finger into Dr. Moe's chest. "If you didn't just pass by the skin of your teeth, we may have gotten into that new dental partnership."

Aunty May separated the two. "Boys, boys. Stop arguing and start making money to get out of debt and move up the dental bridge or ladder."

She laughed at her own joke. She looked around planning the room's configuration with her finger. The two men examined the various rejected furniture. Hans entered the warehouse, stepped among them, and lifted his arms up wide-eyed. Hans then looked at each man and shook his hand. Hans put his hand on the back of Aunty May and massaged her back as they all exited.

With no sign, the warehouse entrance to the dentist office was hidden. A badly scrawled number defaced the faded paint of the door. The warehouse door opened and a housewife with a teenage boy entered. They hesitantly walked up the stairs and looked around. Aunty May sat at an old metal school desk and said, "Good morning. Do you have an appointment?"

The woman who was bug-eyed regarded around the dusty room. She said, "The ad in the newspaper said, 'no appointment necessary.' "

The teenage boy picked at his crooked teeth with his dirty nails, oblivious of his surroundings. Aunty May smiled, "No problem. Or should I ask, what is the problem?"

The woman said, "My son may need braces. Do you have a dentist that can look at him?"

The teenager snooped around the office.

Dr. Lars in a white lab coat stepped from behind a ratty old shower curtain. "Good morning, I'm Dr. Moe Lars. He can come and sit right down."

Dr. Lars pulled his yellowed shower drape aside and pointed to a folding deck chair. Dressed in a grey industrial coat, Dr. Able came out from behind a dusty stained folding screen. "Hello, I'm Dr. Pierce Able. He can come into this area."

The two dentists pulled on either side of the teenager. Wide-mouthed, the teenager wailed, "Mom, look."

They all looked at a small table-saw with teeth on it and pliers. Dr. Lars waved his arm. "There's nothing to worry about."

Dr. Able grinned, "I only do examinations on the first visit."

The woman grabbed her son and started for the door. Aunty May yelled, "Here's a copy of our fee structure when you come back. First visit is free."

Aunty May got up from behind her desk and stood glaring at the two men. They flapped their hands up to the ceiling and slinked into their respective cubicles.

The next day, the outside door opened, and two trashy hos entered. They slowly walked up the stairs and looked around. Bare concrete walls and floor; mismatched furniture.

Aunty May put on a big cheery smile. "Good morning. Do you have an appointment?"

With her frizzy red hair almost matched to her ruby lipstick, the first who spoke, "The ad in the newspaper stated, 'no appointment necessary.' "

The other woman with a sparkly scarf around her hair looked around then laid on the lumpy couch. Her short skirt hiked up to expose her tattered fishnet pull-up stockings.

Aunty May's voice had a condescending tone. "No problem. Or should I ask, what is her problem?" She pointed to the gum-popping reclined tart.

The first lady of the night laughed. "Some of our 'clients' are complaining of her overbite."

The other pulled up her hose to reveal red unmentionables. Both dentists peeked around the corner.

Dr. Moe strode confidently toward the host. "Good morning, I'm Dr. Moe Lars. She can come and sit right down."

Dr. Able rushed out to the standing woman. "Hello, I'm Dr. Pierce Able. You can enter into this area."

The two dentists entered each cubicle with a woman. The first lady stormed out. She shouted, "Cash only. No barter."

Dr. Moe blubbered his reply, "That's not possible at this time."

The whore, smiled mischievously as she walked out. Dr. Pierce said annoyed, "Sorry, I only do oral examinations on the first visit."

The first woman grabbed her companion and started for the door.

Aunty May's voice croaked, "Here's a copy of our fee structure when you come back. First visit free!"

Aunty May stood up and put her hands on her ample hips. Her lips a straight line. The two dentists lifted their coat collars up past their ears and tiptoed into their respective cubicles.

The warehouse door creaked open to bright sunlight and two fashionably dressed young women arrived. Wide-eyed, they cautiously ambled up the stairs littered with papers and grime and beheld around the empty room. The musty air needed freshening.

Aunty May asked, "Good morning. Do you have an appointment?"

In a Boston accent, the first long-lashed young woman said, "The ad in the newspaper said, 'no appointment necessary.' "

The other long-haired young woman looked around smiling then sat demurely on the couch.

Aunty May smiled. "No problem. Or should I ask, what are your problems?"

The first young woman fluttering her fake eye lashes said, "We both want to get into acting and we need our teeth to sparkle." Her teeth were white but needed that special extra.

The other young woman pulled out a mirror from her purse and looked at herself. Both dentists peeked around the shower curtain corner. Dr. Moe walked out upright. "Good morning, I'm Dr. Moe Lars. She can come and sit right down."

Dr. Pierce strode out towards the other young woman. "Hello, I'm Dr. Pierce Able. You can enter into this area."

The two dentists went to their own cubicle with a young woman. The first young woman stormed out red-faced. "You're old enough to be my father."

Dr. Moe's voice quavered. "That's not possible. I'm only 28."

The other young woman dabbed at her eyes with a tissue as she walked out of the cubicle.

Dr. Pierce's voice rose. "Sorry, I didn't mean my mirror to slip onto your lap."

The first young woman grabbed her companion and started for the door.

Aunty May called, "Here's a copy of our fee structure when you come back. First visit free!"

Aunty May stood up from behind her desk and glared at the two men. "That's three incidents. Another and I am out." The two dentists skulked into their respective cubicles.

In the rundown industrial area, the steel warehouse door scraped open and stocky Hans Weiner lumbered in traditional German dress – knee-length leather pants, the haferl shoe with a thick leather or rubber sole, knee-high socks, and a typical Alpine hat, usually made of warm felt or wool. He walked into the back storage of one of the industrial units that he rented out as a dental office.

Hans spoke in his broken German accent, "A great location. You must be having a lot of traffic? Yah?" It was the end of the dental practice's first week.

Aunty May looked at the empty dirty couch. Dr. Moe Lars gazed at the old wooden cabinets piled in the room. "It's a bit early for patients today." It was almost three o'clock.

Aunty May's voice brightened, "But it will fill up shortly."

Dr. Pierce Able rubbed his stubble chin. "We have kept our prices low to start."

Hans went to Dr. Able and thumped him on the chest with a big smile. "Price, price. Yah, you a few days late with your monthly check."

Dr. Moe Lars gave a nervous laugh and looked at his aunt. "Didn't you mail the rent check last week, Aunty May?"

Aunty May nervously smiled up to Hans. Hans spread out his arms around the room. "I gave you good stuff, no charge. I come back Friday with mail."

Grumpy and swearing in German under his breathe, Hans walked past the trio. After the door slammed, the trio looked around. Each descended down the tunnel of despair and uncertainty.

Aunty May said to her nephew, "After putting you through dental school, Moe, I've already lent you the rent deposit."

Dr. Able sat on the couch with the newspaper and beckoned the other two. "Here's an ad in the local newspaper looking for local dentists to service welfare recipients."

Smiling now, Dr. Lars agreed, "At our slow startup speed, we better take on any extra work that we can."

Dr. Able agreed, "Great, we may get into a new dental partnership with the local government."

Aunty May's voice rose, "Boys, boys. Start making money and move up the dental bridge or ladder." She croaked at her little joke.

The two men patted each other on the back and shook hands. They grabbed a pad of paper and conferred what to put in their application letter – truth or dare.

Chapter 2 - LOOKING FOR A NEW PARTNER

In a small government office cubicle, Dr. Pierce Able saw a middle-aged woman sitting at her paper-mountain-piled-desk reading some documents. Looking at the name plate, *Miss Money-Pennyless*, Dr. Pierce Able slicked back his stringy hair and practiced his suave smile before knocking at the corner of her cubicle. The woman looked up and smiled at him with crooked teeth. Her multi-flounced outfit deflated like a spent balloon as she stood up and shook his hand.

"Come in and sit down Dr. Able," she said. "Thank you for coming in and taking time from your busy schedule."

Dr. Able tried to sit down but the seat was covered with files which Miss Money-Pennyless then snatched away and put on the floor beside her.

Dr. Able chuckled, "Thank you, Miss Money-Pennyless. An unusual name."

"Hmm." Miss Money-Pennyless scowled. "Yes, an old family name from over the pond. Now, you are here to sign up for the new dental health incentive?"

Dr. Able rubbed his chin. "Yes, I am. But I have a few small questions."

Miss Money-Pennyless beamed as she bent over her desk to hand him a thick shiny covered book. "Good,

good. They will probably all be answered in this 500-page volume of government practices and procedures."

Dr. Able's eyes widened. "Yes, I've seen those texts. My question is about payment."

"Now don't you worry about payment by the government." Miss Money-Pennyless winked, her slate-grey curls bounced. "They always pay within 180 days."

Dr. Able gritted his uneven teeth – not all dentists have the best teeth.

"Well, I have just started up my practice and I am a bit short..." he muttered. *Drat to my unsuccessful internet gambling.*

She leaned closer to him, pulled down her wrinkled, sagging cleavage and gave him another wink. She tapped the inside of her hand.

"You're a bright young man." she cooed in a voice too young and sexy for her years. "I'm quite sure we can come to a mutual and satisfying arrangement."

He leaned away from her with disgust. Her thin rouge-red flyaway hair, puffy bags under her eyes, and dried riverbed face. The smell of dried-up dusting powder.

"I seem to have no choice," Dr. Able choked.

She grabbed his arm tightly, pulled him towards her and laughingly whispered in his ear. Dr. Able rolled his bloodshot eyes. *What did he get himself into? This was a down and dirty price to pay for his obsessions.*

The warehouse door opened to the dental practice and a large muscular guy in a wife-beater shirt entered bobbing to his headphones. He jive-walked up the stairs and looked around.

"Good morning," Aunty May beamed cheerfully. "You are early!"

He nodded his head in tempo. An older man, Mr. Bender, watched from where he sat on the couch.

"Are you the ten o'clock appointment?" Aunty May asked.

The music man shook his head 'no'. The beads in his dreadlocks knocked against each other.

"Are you the eleven o'clock appointment?"

The dark-skinned music man again shook his head 'no.'

"Do you have an appointment?" Aunty May smiled back at him.

For the third time, the music man nodded his head 'no'. He walked up to the receptionist and pulled out a wad of bills from his pocket. Aunty May's eyes widened.

"Now I remember. You have an emergency appointment." The music man shook his head 'yes'. He leaned over and showed the large gaping cavity in his back molar.

Dr. Moe walked into the room, escorting an older woman out of his office.

"Next time you run out of dental floss, don't use knitting yarn." He warned as the woman walked up to Aunty May Lars to pay her bill.

"Who is next?" Dr. Moe asked. The older man in his ankle-length pants showing wrinkled yellowed socks stood up and took a step toward the dentist.

While writing up a receipt, Aunty May called out in a loud voice, "I'm sorry Mr. Bender, but you will have to wait a few more minutes."

Shrugging to the older man, Dr. Moe Lars escorted the jiving man into his cubicle. Mr. Bender hobbled over to the receptionist, his hand on his back rubbing a kink.

He croaked, "I see that lots of money saves time. I've spent too much time here, so you won't get my money." Mr. Bender waddled out in a huff. "Seniors don't get preferential treatment!"

Dr. Moe Lars walked out a short time later with the satisfied music man and looked around for Mr. Bender. Aunty May shook her head.

Dr. Moe Lars said, "That's too bad Mr. Bender was in such a hurry since I am now free." He shrugged as he looked at the empty sitting area. "Some seniors are so impatient."

Later that day, the warehouse door screeched open and Hans Weiner, their landlord, entered. He walked and stood in front of the trio of Aunty May, Dr. Lars, and Dr. Pierce. In his German accent he bellowed, "You having traffic yet? Yah?"

Aunty May looked at the empty stained lumpy sofa. Dr. Moe nervously laughed. "We will have more patients in the afternoon."

Aunty May thumped down in her rickety wooden chair. Her faded cotton dress billowed around her rotund figure. Her unwashed odor wafted around her.

"It will fill up shortly," she confirmed.

Dr. Pierce replied wide-grinned, "We are friendly and efficient."

Hans went to him and pulled out envelopes from his pocket. "Late with your rent check. Yeah?"

Dr. Moe's voice rose into a squeak. "Aunty May?" *She had better save them again.*

Aunty May nervously smiled up to Hans who then turned to her handbag under the desk. Hans narrowed his eyes as he took the check. "I no charge you for late this time."

Sneering, Hans walked past the trio. After the door closed, the trio looked around at their bare and squalor surroundings.

Aunty May pulled out a tissue from her purse and dabbed her eyes, "After putting you through dental school, Moe, I won't be able to pay my own month's rent."

Grabbing the newspaper off of the couch, Dr. Pierce said, "Let's put an ad in the community newspaper to look for local dentists to sublet this space after hours."

Aunty May loudly blew her nose. "So, that local government dental scheme didn't pan out?"

With a cough, Dr. Pierce was guarded, "No, no. I guess we weren't experienced enough."

Dr. Moe's voice brightened, "At our slow startup speed, we better take on any subcontractors that we can."

Dr. Pierce cheered, "Great! We may get into a new dental partnership with an experienced dentist."

Aunty May sat up straight. "Boys, boys. Start finding money wherever you can, or we are out of here."

As she got back to her paperwork, the two men sat down on the couch with a pen and pad to design a persuasive ad.

The next day, the warehouse door whooshed opened and a three-piece, black-suited man entered. He walked up the stairs looking around in awe. A young man sat on the couch lecherously eyeing and winking at a sexy woman in a revealing top. The trio of Aunty May, Dr. Moe and Dr. Pierce stood beside the woman.

In a huff, Aunty May replied, "It may be a while before someone takes over my job."

Dr. Moe viewed his aunt from the corner of his eye and gave the hot young thing a secret wink.

"I'll let you know when we can hire an assistant," he looked at her with delight.

Aunty May brightened as she looked at the handsome man who had entered. "Oh, do we have another patient?"

The young woman stood up and tapped Dr. Moe's chest.

"Don't take too long or someone else will take advantage of my assets," she cooed.

With a wiggle of her hips and her cleavage, the woman started down the steps, watched the handsome man pass her, and then hesitated. The man approached the desk.

Dr. Pierce looked at him, "I'm not busy I can take you now."

The man's eyes wrinkled. "No, I'm here to look at your location for the dental night shift as per your ad in the newspaper. My name is Dr. Teddy Tooth."

He opened his mouth and his teeth gleamed as sparkling as mountain river water. His breath was minty clean. Dr. Moe, Aunty May and Dr. Pierce gathered around.

Dr. Moe stepped closer, "I can give you a private tour."

Dr. Pierce grabbed his arm. "Mine will be more comprehensive."

The man took one step forward, bending from the waist looking around – dirty ripped couch; one step to the right, observing – a marked wooden school-desk for a reception; two steps to the left, peering – a shower curtain divider in the dental service area; one step to the back and he stood up straight – piles of lumber and debris in all the corners.

Dr. Teddy Tooth's mouth was a beacon of light. "I've seen enough. No, thank you."

He walked down the stairs blocked by the young woman.

She fluttered her eyelashes, "Excuse me, sir. Are you a real dentist?"

He nodded. She put her arm in his and they stepped out.

As they exited, Dr. Moe, Aunty May and Dr. Pierce chided each other as the warehouse door opened and a courier man entered. He walked up the stairs looking around suspiciously.

Dressed in his brown uniform, the courier shuffled, "I had a hard time finding this place."

Dr. Moe pointed to the bare door, "Our sign is being made next door."

Aunty May handed him the parcel. "Here's our parcel."

The man passed her an invoice. "Since you haven't been in business for six months, it must be pre-paid."

She begrudgingly filled in the form and handed him a check. As he went out the door, a different courier man came in. "That's good I saw the last guy coming out, I couldn't locate the place."

Dr. Pierce was annoyed, "I'll go next door and find out what's taking them so long with the sign." *Good help is hard to find.*

The second courier man in his green outfit looked at the parcel,

"This parcel is COD please."

The courier man handed her a slip of paper that she filled in and handed him a check. As he left, Dr. Moe spoke gingerly, "More checks out than money in."

Aunty May Lars slammed the checkbook close and put it in the drawer.

A short time later the warehouse door opened, and a bag woman entered. With matted greasy hair and a dirty face, she walked up the stairs and squinted into the box strewn corners. The trio of Aunty May, Dr. Moe

and Dr. Pierce stood a few feet away from the bag lady as she plopped on the sagging couch. They waved their hands in front of their noses. An odor combination of butt wipe, old ketchup, and unwashed.

Aunty May coughed, "We will call you about your next appointment." *Please leave now.*

The bag lady slurred through her missing teeth, "But I don't have a phone. Someone told me you were looking for new patients."

Dr. Moe raised his voice. "Yes, new patients but a different type of patient." *Yes, clean, and neat.*

Aunty May covered her nose with a tissue as another bag lady entered. "Oh, we have another one of those patients." *Can it get any worse?*

The second bag lady stuck out her lower jaw to show her one wobbly tooth and slurred, "I don't feel so bad now, I know someone."

In her ratty, matted, fur coat with used tissues hanging out, she plunked on the seat beside the other woman. The first bag lady touched the other's coat sleeve of many layers and dust pooled out.

"Ethel, I haven't seen you in a dog's age," the first bag lady spoke in her muffled voice.

Dr. Pierce staggered back from the garbage-can smell. "I'm busy right now so it may be a while." *Let me out of here!*

Dr. Moe Lars pinched his thin nose. The combined odors become stifling.

"I need to fumigate my office and sanitize my hands so you can take her," gasped Dr. Moe Lars. *I'm going to take a very long time.*

The two doctors squeezed their noses with one hand while pointing to each other and shaking their heads. Crumbs fell away from the second bag lady's clothes.

"Don't hurry Doctors. We have a lot of catching up to do," the second bag lady got comfortable.

The two doctors ran into their cubicles as Aunty May stood up and sprayed an air freshener.

The warehouse door opened, and a professional-looking man entered. He walked up the stairs looking around suspiciously at the two women on the couch, the air spraying and the two men huddled in their cubicles.

Aunty May sneezed. "I'll be right with you."

The man in the tailored suit looked around, "This isn't a proper dental office, it's a ..."

Before speaking anymore, he put his hand to his mouth, gagged and ran out.

The next morning when the door opened, a woman entered wearing a navy three-piece suit, white frilly blouse, and matching navy purse and shoes. She walked up the stairs looking around wide-eyed.

The trio of Aunty May, Dr. Moe Lars and Dr. Pierce stood beside a young blind woman, Connie. Her brown curly hair framed her porcelain oval face as she leaned on her white cane.

Aunty May asked, "Shall I make your next appointment for Monday?"

Dr. Moe Lars held onto the woman's arm a bit too long.

"I'll be able to start work on your cleaning," Dr. Moe Lars using his best voice. *Maybe other things.*

Aunty May looked up with a smile, "Oh, do we have another patient?"

Pulling her arm away from Dr. Moe Lars, Connie smiled, "I'm so glad I found your friendly office."

Connie started down the steps. The other woman approached the desk. Dr. Pierce licked his thin lips at the new woman's fit figure.

"I'm not busy I can take you now," Dr. Pierce grinned. *In more ways than one.*

The woman gave him the look. "No, I'm here to look at your location for the dental night shift as per your ad in the newspaper. My name is Dr. Wilma Wisdom."

Dr. Moe Lars, Aunty May and Dr. Pierce gathered around her a little too close. Dr. Moe rubbed his chin.

"I can give you a private tour," Dr. Moe Lars spoke with his devilish smile. *My place would be even better.*

Dr. Pierce pushed him aside. "Mine will be more comprehensive." *I know how to please a woman.*

Dr. Wilma Wisdom sneered in disgust. "I've seen enough." *Perverts.*

With a strong wind howling outside the warehouse, the entrance door took brute strength before Miss Money-Pennyless could enter. She squinted in the low light as she walked up the stairs. Dr. Pierce Able, looking disgruntled, furiously typed on a laptop on a side table. Miss Money-Pennyless tiptoed up to him and put her clammy hands around his eyes. Dr. Pierce jumped and slammed down the computer. An avalanche of papers flew over the floor. *What the…*

Aunty May and Dr. Moe entered from the back and rushed onto the scene. Miss Money-Pennyless gasped with her hand to her chest.

"I'm so sorry, Dr. Pierce Able. I didn't mean to startle you," Miss Money-Pennyless looking vaguely concerned.

Aunty May looked the rotund woman with the pancake hat up and down. "Good afternoon. Do you have an appointment?"

Miss Money-Pennyless gave a shrill laugh. "No appointment. I'm Miss Money-Pennyless from the city public health department."

Dr. Moe Lars nervously looked around. "Health department? Our landlord, Hans Weiner, assured us all our permits and licenses are in order." *What trouble are we in now?*

Miss Money-Pennyless waved her arthritic-bent finger at him. "No, no. I'm not from that city department. But from the one that deals with the dental scam, I mean scheme," she looked around the office.

Aunty May looked puzzled. "I thought we weren't accepted in that dental scam, I mean scheme."

Dr. Pierce's voice rose a few octaves. "Didn't I tell you? Hee, hee. The paperwork has just come through." *EEK! How am I going to fix this?*

Miss Money-Pennyless rubbed her chin. "Oh, I see... I didn't know Dr. Pierce worked with another dentist."

Dr. Moe Lars and Aunty May glared at Dr. Pierce. Dr. Moe Lars spoke up, "Yes, right from the beginning. We're partners."

Miss Money-Pennyless grinned. "Oh. You must be the silent partner. I'll just go out to my car and get you the paperwork to get you into this dental scam, I mean scheme."

All three watched Miss Money-Pennyless exit. Aunty May's eyes narrowed at Dr. Pierce. "You couldn't come with us for lunch because of your paperwork."

She grabbed the papers out of his hand and shuffled through them. "You promised no more Internet gambling."

Dr. Moe Lars paced back and forth. "You probably spent all the money you, 'scammed'"

Aunty May made a show of wiping her hands together. "Boys, the well has run dry. The rent is due in a few days and you're on your own."

Aunty May left the front office as the dentists had their hands flailing, heads shaking and loud shouting at each other.

The full moon lit up like an antique lantern that night. The warehouse door opened without a squeak or groan as a towering, raven-haired man in a dark, black, flowing cape entered. He didn't walk up the stairs – he seemed to float up to the landing as he looked around. The trio of Aunty May, Dr. Moe, and Dr. Pierce stood beside seated petit Connie.

Aunty May asked, "Shall I make your next appointment for Friday?" Connie nodded. She straightened her dark glasses.

Dr. Moe Lars drew a little closer, "I'll be able to start work on that back molar." *Among other things.*

Aunty May looked towards the entrance. "Oh, do we have another patient?"

Connie stood up with her white cane and waved, "Goodbye now."

Tapping her cane, Connie started down the steps and tripped. The tall man turned, grabbed her hand, and helped her to steady herself.

"You have such cool hands."

The tall man looked at her beautiful rosy skin. "Yes, I can feel your hot blood," in a silky whisper.

The man tipped his tall silk black hat as he watched her exit out the door then went up to the desk. Dr. Pierce looked cautiously at the death-grey pallor of the man.

"I'm not busy I can take you now," Dr. Pierce spoke, a rough tone to his voice.

The tall man's thin pale lips curved back to show gleaming ivory fangs. "No, I'm here to look at your location for the dental night shift, as per your ad in the newspaper. My name is Dr. Drek Vam Dent." His voice was iceberg cold.

Dr. Moe, Aunty May and Dr. Pierce all gave a chorused gasp then gathered around the mesmerizing figure with the red piercing eyes.

Chapter 3 - *NEW DENTAL PARTNERSHIP*

Dr. Vam Dent looked around at the rundown location – a flattened soiled couch, broken chairs, and old tattered magazines on a coffee-stained veneer table.

Dr. Pierce Able coughed then shrilled his voice, "And how will you be paying your partnership rental fee?" *Yah. Where does this creep get his money?*

Dr. Vam Dent's eyes glowed. He reached into his pocket and pulled out some gold coins and placed them on the table. "My clients pay with their ethereal resources. Let these coins be a down payment."

Dr. Able leaned forward but Auntie May was faster. Her eyes reflected the shiny monies. "I'll be able to pay my bills and last month's rent on this deposit. I look forward to our partnership." She stuck out her hand then quickly drew it back. Dr. Vam Dent's eyes glowed redder.

Dr. Moe Lars' voice was high pitched. "When will your clients be arriving?"

Dr. Van Dent closed his eyes and looked skyward. "Word is out now. Tomorrow will be the first night's dental service."

Dr. Lars brought in a breath. "I'll stay late tomorrow to get you acquainted with our procedures."

Aunty Mae looked at him, "I'll have your receipt for you tomorrow and our partnership agreement. The bookkeeping will be included in the monthly rent."

Dr. Van Dent spread his hands and motioned toward the office, "All I ask for is full access from dusk to dawn for myself and my clients."

Dr. Moe Lars glared at Dr. Able's silence. "That suits me, Dr. Moe Lars and Dr. Piece Able, my partner."

"My Aunty Mae Lars is our office manager." Dr. Able nodded.

Dr. Able's fingers flexed in frustration. He stuck them in his white overcoat pockets. *I'll have to check on his patient's payments on a regular basis. Maybe take some excess for myself.*

The Vam Dent family is a royal family from the Transylvanian region of Romania – a long, long time ago. There was a terrible plague in our land. The only way to prolong ourselves was to go to the dark side with the original Shadow Attackers from the north. Many of the royal families took the bite, many did not, and died. Not all royal families in the ring of the Carpathian Mountains got along – petty and juvenile fighting. These disruptions continued with our new eternal forms.

Eternal life had its own consequences with our constant blood feeding. Many years later, even though we left the motherland because of persecution, we were able to take with us our jewelry, coinage, and some favored artwork and paintings. At times, we may have to barter or exchange our valuables for more mundane items or services.

As a royal family, the Vam Dents, we don't need to increase our family. Someone has to be very special to be turned into a vampire into our family. We prefer to just suck enough blood to sustain ourselves. We may seek out our former victims to indulge again. We have learned in the past that we cannot leave dead bodies for the authorities to find and track us down. It's best that the victims appear to be sick or injured and that is why they are low on their blood supply.

Our Vam Dent family likes to stick together for both company and protection. We still have enemies from the motherland, the Shadow Attackers, and the local authorities.

Once we become vampires, our aging stops. But like any material, the skin is susceptible to the ravages of sunlight, wind, cold, and heat. Since the body is basically death, we must be aware of mildew, bacteria, and viruses attacking the skin. A hot red wine bath gets rid of any pests. This should be done on a semi-annual basis. Any stage of the wine will suffice.

As for sleeping, we don't need to be rejuvenated – only blood satisfies us. The longer our hunger, the more vicious could be our attacks. Sometimes it takes more than one human to satisfy us.

Climate and Weather don't affect us vampires. Rain, snow, and sleet may wet us, but any warmer air will take care of drying of our clothes. We don't respond to heat or cold. Our hands, face, and flesh feel cold to the touch. Except acid rain can put holes in our old outer clothes. We cannot influence the weather – but somehow the wind...

We vampires drink warm human blood. Only under dire circumstances will we drain a dead person or an animal. If we drain all the blood from a human, they die. If we only drain a portion, that means that we may have them as a food source for later. Or, we may want to turn them into vampires and into our family clan if they are special enough.

As per our past lives as humans, we enjoyed a good bottle of wine and gourmet foods. Now, we may taste it just for remembrance. Our bodies can only consume human blood. We do not have an elimination system or sweat. Our hunger is the greatest during a full moon.

Since our Vam Dent family was elevated to vampires in centuries past, many of our clothes are from that era. We may look a lot like Goths to some people. Since we don't sweat or perspire, there is no need to change clothes.

Our hair and nails don't grow because we are dead. No need for haircuts. The women vampires may want to get their hair done or wear wigs or extensions. They may enjoy manicures and pedicures. Most of our royal women like to dress up in their finery and jewels. Wearing makeup isn't necessary unless you want your skin to be more alive-like to pursue someone with less fright.

Chapter 5 - GREENHOUSE ATTACKS

The many glass greenhouses were on an old family Gage estate that was donated to the city. Their white painted glass windows were colored with years of leaves from the surrounding trees. The grey aluminum glass frames were twisted from battering of wind, rain, sleet, and snow. A few times a year there, the city hosted flower displays by season or celebration.

It was evening, and her work still wasn't done. An 18-year-old greenhouse attendant, Brittany, in denim britches, swept a few bits of crushed and curled brown foliage into a pile.

With his black cape billowing behind him, the male vampire, Andrain, moved stealthfully down the center of the greenhouse. *Mmmm, a young worker. Fresh with rapidly pumping blood. The easier to suck.*

The woman worker bent over to pick up the litter pile on the floor with a broom and dustbin. The heavy smell of plant rot would have offended most. The whirling of the wall exhaust fan deadened any footsteps – if they were human. As her head lifted up and she saw the vampire, her eyes widened and her mouth cavernous in a silent scream.

The vampire roughly grabbed her by the shoulders and lifted her from her bent posture. She swooned with eyes rolling back in her head. Her blond hair flopped to the side. The vampire bared his yellow, decayed fangs and moved in. The sucking noise stopped when he laid her prone on the ground – her skin as white and grey and almost cold as the concrete floor she lay on.

That same night, a middle-aged woman, Glenda, with her copper-haired young son, Raymond, walked into a greenhouse of dying chrysanthemums – white, yellow, and orange colors – now tinged in brown decay with so many petals falling away. The smell of flower rot in the air. The two didn't know that the greenhouse chrysanthemum show was over that day and that the doors were now locked to visitors.

But the facility was not empty. Two young and cocky male vampires, Emmanmaul and Peels, had concealed themselves at the back of one greenhouse behind some wooden plant crates. Their black capes concealed them like shadows.

The family looked at and touched with quivering fingers the dying brown flowers.

The woman's voice insulted, "I've seen fresher flowers at a graveyard's compost heap."

The young man's eyes bulged. His nostrils flared and lips pinched straight. The back of his neck prickled. He sensed something BAD. "We must have wandered into the wrong area." *Oh no!*

Then Glenda's voice heightened. "I'll raise the dead to demand a partial refund."

They had concentrated too much on the dead flowers and didn't see the two male vampires' approach. Emmanmaul's black shiny hair looked more like a mannequin's wig than that of an age-old blood sucker. He grabbed the plump woman. Her ivory skin was cool to the touch in these unheated greenhouses. But her cheeks were flushed. The full flush of fright and the temptation of rich wine-colored blood.

"Run, run!" she screamed.

Peels, the dark-skinned blood scrounger, always wanted to taste a ginger. The boy's breath was coming in gasps. That did not help blood circulation and his face was ashen ivory. "Ma, help, help!" he screamed. When the youth's eyes rolled back into his head, Peels jumped forward to lay him on his side to expose the neck.

Sucking and slurping sounds were masked by the two victims' high and echoing screams.

Blind Connie's apartment lay between the industrial mall and the park with the greenhouses. At dusk, Connie sat on her bed putting on her sweater. A knock at the apartment door confused her.

"Who is it?"

She moved toward the door and opened it. She could tell who it was by the smell of hand disinfectant. "Dr. Moe Lars — I wasn't expecting you."

Dr. Moe Lars rubbed his hands nervously. "I was in the area so I thought I would drop by. You left your wallet in the office."

Connie's lips pursed. "Oh, thank you. I was on my way to the greenhouses in the park. I heard that they have a mum show on now."

His eyes twinkled. "May I escort you there?"

Connie drew out a long breath. "Sorry, Dr. Lars, but I am meeting Dr. Vam Dent there."

Moe grimaced, then smiled. "I can escort you at least to the door."

She said, "Oh no. I have to refresh myself before I go and do a few chores. Why don't I just meet you there?" *I definitely don't want to encourage him.*

Shoulders hunched, he turned to leave. "Oh, OK. I'll see you there."

In the darkness, Drek Vam Dent, with his long black silk cape billowing, walked up the path towards the main doors of the tropical greenhouse with its broken panes and rusty hinges. He easily opened the door and entered.

From a distance, Dr. Moe Lars spied Drek's movements. Moe sneaked up the path and casually pulled on the metal door handle. *What the …*

The door did not open. He pulled harder and harder – the muscles in his hands tensed. Moe slinked back along the path and viewed another door. *Hmm, how did he get in?*

He pulled at this door, but it was also locked. He turned and looked back at the first door. Hand on hip, he scratched his head. *There must be a trick.*

He strode back to the first door, bent down, put both hands on the doorknob, yanked with all his might and almost fell down as the door opened with no trouble.

Inside the tropical greenhouse, Connie walked along the path tapping her white cane back and forth. She stopped, bent over, and smelt the flowers. Geraniums, Impatiens, Petunias, Ferns, Poinsettias, Chrysanthemums. The air was warm, humid, and earthy.

Drek Vam Dent stepped out of the shadows and put his heavily veined hand on her pump ivory hand.

Connie gasped. "Oh, Dr. Vam Dent. Your hand is so cool and firm. You are making me flush." *I never heard or smelled him approaching.*

Drek slid his fingers on her hand and slowly and seductively moved his digits up her arm. "The flush of the rose is on your neck."

Connie cocked her head and drew in a breath. "The flowers in this room are mums, aren't they? Not roses?"

Drek moved closer to her neck. "I need to smell your rose's flush." He slowly licked her neck.

Connie moaned and lifted her head up. He stepped back from her and bared his fangs. He slowly moved toward her neck.

The door to the tropical greenhouse burst open and Dr. Moe Lars entered. Moe saw Drek's head poised near Connie's neck.

He called out, "Hey Drek! Is her perfume better than the smell of all these dead mums?"

Drek still had his back to Moe who joined the couple. Unscathed, Connie moved away from Drek. "Pardon me, gentlemen. I must find the ladies' room." *That was totally unexpected.*

She straightened her clothing then tapped along the slate path with her cane. *My knees are rubbery.*

Both men watched her leave the tropical greenhouse. Moe spoke up, "Isn't she lovely? I'd like to put the bite on her."

Drek's eyes burned red. "Maybe another time. Adieu."

Moe stood looking where Connie had exited. Drek swept his cape around him and left the tropical house.

Outside in the park, the air was still cool, and heady, with fallen autumn leaves. An owl called from the trees. From the gate of the fenced enclosure, Connie walked along the lighted path tapping her white cane back and forth. *I better get back home before I can't control herself with Drek.*

Dr. Moe Lars, standing halfway down the path, watched her approach. "Hey, Miss Connie. Did he give you the slip?" He moved closer to her.

Connie hesitated, "Oh, Dr. Moe Lars. I guess Dr. Vam Dent is very busy with his new practice and must get back." *Like me home, away from Moe.*

Connie tripped and started to fall forward. Moe grabbed her arm. "Easy does it now."

She straightened up and took his hand off her arm. " Dr. Lars, your hand is so warm, clammy, and soft." *Yuk!*

Moe stuck his hands into his pockets. "I do wash them a lot. What about going for a coffee, Miss Connie?"

She walked past him. "No thank you. I don't know why I am so tired." *And his smell nauseates me.*

He kicked the path as he saw her walk away.

Connie walked up the stairs of the rundown, triplex house where she lived to the paint-peeling front door with its low-wattage bulb. She hesitated and cocked her head from side-to-side straining to hear. With her eyesight gone, her hearing was acute, but she couldn't identify the unusual sounds. She opened the brown, wood-splintered door and entered.

Connie walked up the thread-bare carpeted stairs going up from the first level. Dust swirled at each of her steps from the old dirty worn carpet. She sneezed. She stopped and listened. It wasn't a knocking; it wasn't a tapping; it wasn't a humming.

At the second level, Connie closed the door behind her then walked up the stairs to the third level attic. She didn't notice the grey cobwebs in the corner, the dirty small window, and the peeled paint, but she smelled the mold, mildew, and dust.

On the landing, she paused again and tilted her head from side-to-side straining to hear. At the top of the stairs, she turned as if looking at the closed door to her apartment. Was there a hand pressed to the door on the other side?

Connie walked into the apartment toward the lacy white lamp on the bedside table and turned it on. Her attic window was left open a pinch. The south attic door opened a crack. A grey smoke swirled into the room.

She removed her jacket and put it on a chair. The north attic door opened a crack. A cool wind whooshed out.

She took off her blouse and skirt leaving her in her virgin-white underwear and slip. The closet door opened a crack. A red wrinkled eye looked out.

Connie moved towards her bed. All three doors opened at once with three male vampires about to pounce.

A loud knock startled Connie and she grabbed her white robe off the bed. "Who is it?" All three attic doors closed silently.

Connie opened the stairway door to reveal Dr. Drek standing on the landing. His voice was low and throaty. "I'm sorry, I know it is late."

He sniffed the air. He entered her apartment. He approached each of the other three doorknobs and turned them slightly then pushed them in. "I've had some bad people following me and I wanted to make sure you were safe."

She placed her hand on her forehead. "I'm sorry but I am very tired after my walk through the greenhouse." *Oh, no. He's in my bedroom.*

Drek's red piercing eyes rounded as they beheld her voluptuous figure in the virginal white lingerie. "Another night for a longer visit." He looked at all three doorknobs.

After Connie closed the door behind him, she lay under the bed's covers. The other three doorknobs turned slightly one way then went back. Her sleep that night was disturbing, and it wasn't just about the attic doors.

The full moon shone bright as a young woman in her quilted, flowered housecoat walked down the cracked, asphalt driveway of Connie's triplex house with a trash bag in her hand. She went over to the dirty fractured plastic garbage can, opened the lid and dropped the bag in.

When she bent over, three male vampires grabbed her on all sides and swooped in for the bite. Andrain flipped back his wavy blond hair; Peels wiped his black bald head; Emmanmaul scrunched his Oriental eyes.

Screaming and struggling, she fainted limp on the ground as they dragged her away. Her brown hair tangled, her pink nightgown under her housecoat askew with her legs dangling. They had lost one tasty morsel in the attic. They now found one on the ground.

Chapter 6 - HUMAN PATIENTS

Even though now they had a new nighttime dentist paying them rent, the human patients during the day still had to be serviced. Three people sat on a couch reading magazines – a man between two women. Nearby, the receptionist, Auntie Mae Lars, worked on her paperwork.

Dr. Moe Lars walked up to the three. "Which rose should I take next?"

One woman stood up and waved her hand in front of her nose. A putrid smell came from somewhere on the couch. Her dark skin was highlighted by her bright yellow blouse. "It better be me."

Dr. Moe Lars inhaled the fragrance, "Yes, you do smell nice." He looked at the other two. "Now don't let that man prick you."

The other woman, older with self-cut grey bangs and a curly mop of hair, moved to the arm of the couch. "As long as you don't jab, I'll wait for you." Her long billowing white blouse hid more than her curves.

The young, pimply-faced man buried himself behind his magazine. His long bulbous nose didn't smell anything nice about her.

From the receptionist's desk, a tall rakish young woman approached the grimy couch where two men sat at each end. She looked at the middle, then at each arm of the couch. She sat in the middle after pulling down her short skirt. The two men edged closer to her. One man's large, rough, cracked hands clenched in and out while the shorter man's large ears turned to hear better. Nearby, Auntie Mae Lars worked on her paperwork oblivious of the goings-on.

Dr. Moe Lars walked up to the three. "Which rose should I take next?"

The woman tried to stand up and put her hand over her mouth. "It better be me."

"Yes, you do seem a bit cramped." He pulled her up beside him. He looked at the other two, stepped forward and pushed them apart. The couch exhaled a big creak.

"Now that's better. Good men, like wine, need to breathe."

A slapped-sound like two hands against each other resounded between the two men. The men moved to each arm of the couch. Dr. Lars and the young woman entered his cubicle.

Two women on the couch read magazines as Dr. Moe Lars walked up to the two. "Which rose should I pick next?"

Dressed in short-shorts and a bikini top, the blonde bombshell stood up and waved her hand. "I can go next."

Dr. Pierce Able walked out of his cubicle. He grabbed the arm of the first woman and helped up from the couch the second woman, her figure camouflaged in a long black paisley tunic. The women grabbed him around each arm. "I can pluck this rose bush." His chin hairs bristled.

Dr. Moe Lars stomped his feet and threw up his arms as the three entered Dr. Able's cubicle. Auntie Mae Lars clucked her disapproval.

Three people sat on a couch reading magazines – a woman between two men, one holding his swollen cheek. Dr. Moe Lars carrying an aluminum tray, walked up to the three. "Which patient is next?"

The woman with her fine hair standing out like a pin cushion's needles stood up and looked into the tray and saw large pliers and a wire brush. "It won't be me."

She dashed out as the two men looked on. From around the corner, Dr. Pierce Able pulled a rusty vacuum cleaner.

"Dr. Lars, I need this for the next patient. Do you have a cloth I can wipe it off?"

The other disheveled man in a jogging outfit stood up and looked at his watch. "Sorry, I forgot another appointment." He departed quickly.

Dr. Lars handed the lone seated man with the exposed beer belly the tray. "Now don't let the new tools fool you. It's all in the technique." Dr. Lars pulled the groaning man into his cubicle.

Later that afternoon, three women sat on the sagging couch flipping through magazines. Dr. Pierce Able walked up to the three and handed one an aluminum tray. "I will be back in a moment."

He went around the corner of the dingy concrete block room. Each woman took out an item from the tray: a large flashlight, a hefty imperfect magnifying glass, and an ornate plastic hand mirror.

Dr. Able approached the women with a pile of long thin wooden sticks. "OK. I hope you haven't spit on them or anything. I will have to sterilize them again."

He took the jittery young blonde woman into his cubicle behind a ripped plastic shower curtain. A loud scream was followed by the woman running out.

Dr. Lars came out of his cubicle and took one of the other older nervous women, her head wrapped in a bright turban into his cubicle. The woman ran out wide-mouthed.

Dr. Lars came out holding a wire brush. "It's not as rough as it looks."

On the grubby couch, the third woman, the oldest with a gaping and drooling mouth, smiled and winked. "I like dentists' offices and pain." Dr. Lars gave her a demented smile.

The next day, three people sat on the divan – a man between two women, getting friendly and laughing. Dust swirled in the sunlight from the upper window. Nearby, Auntie Mae smiled as she worked on her paperwork.

Wearing a clear plastic hat on his head and yellow rubber gloves, Dr. Moe Lars walked up to the three of them. "Sorry to break up your party."

Looking at Dr. Lars, one woman in a denim jumpsuit laughed loudly and stood up. Dr. Pierce Able came out of his cubicle with a dotted shower cap on his head and large green gardening gloves and grabbed the first woman.

Dr. Lars looked at the other two. The other woman in cotton slacks and a striped top laughed. "As long as you're only cleaning my teeth, I'll come with you." He led the second laughing woman into his cubicle.

Holding the tattered magazines against his ears, the bald-headed man in the wrinkled polyester green suit now left alone, buried his face into the pictures and articles.

Passing the receptionist's small wooden desk, an older man, distinguished with his salt and pepper hair, approached a couch where two women sat at each end. He looked at the sagging middle, then at each worn arm of the chesterfield. He sat in the middle depression and the two young blonde women edged closer to him.

Two young men, obvious construction workers with their dirty jumpsuits and hard hats, entered the dilapidated dental office and saw the two women squeezing the older man. One young man with his front tooth missing said, "Girls, girls. I think you need some fresh air.

Each young man grabbed the hand of a young woman and pulled her up from the couch. Each young woman curled her arm around each young man, and they exited. Both dentists entered the empty scene and looked around.

Dr. Moe Lars stood in the doorway, "You are my next patient."

Dr. Pierce Able stepped aggressively toward the man and quickly opened the man's mouth and saw the ragged teeth and sneered. He and the man entered Dr. Lars' cubicle with the wobbly lawn chair.

An unusual looking man, bearded with a long nose, bushy eyebrows, and hollow cheeks, approached a couch where two men dressed in tennis whites sat at each end. He looked at the middle, then at each arm of the couch. He sat in the middle and the two men edged farther from him.

Dr. Moe Lars walked up to the three. "Which thorn, I mean man, should I take next?"

The unusual man leaped up and leaned forward. "I like pain. A lot of pain."

Dr. Moe Lars chuckled. "OK. No gas for you, I guess."

The unusual man looked at the other two men, stepped forward and wagged a finger at them. "You are next, and I will watch."

The first man in his pressed white shorts and tee shirt gulped. "Watch, watch, look at the time." He ran out.

The other man with a dirty brown cowboy hat sat up straight and beamed thumbs up. "I'm a man; I can take it."

Dr. Lars and the unusual man entered his cubicle. Dr. Able took the second man into his cubicle with the loose tilting office chair.

At another day, three people sat reading magazines – a woman between two men, one holding a thick string dangling from his mouth. Dr. Moe Lars walked up to the three and handed them each a baby's bib.
"I'll be right back. Please tie each other up."

The woman with a multi-colored flounce blouse jerked up and threw her bib on the couch. "Is he psychic?

How does he know I'm pregnant?" She left crying as the two men looked on.

From around the corner, Dr. Pierce Able pulled a tall gas cylinder. "Dr. Lars, I need this for the next patient. Do you have a cloth I can wipe it off?"

The other man in rubber boots jumped up and rubbed his stomach. "Sorry, I have enough gas from lunch." He flew out the door.

Holding under his armpit a large industrial blue paper towel roll, Dr. Lars grabbed the seated man with the string. "Now don't worry. I'll wipe up any drool."

Chapter 7 - PARK ATTACKS

Outside of the greenhouse and tropical house in the Gage Park, many trees and bushes made cozy hiding places for the fang group to attack night human visitors or park residents.

The male Oriental vampire, Emmanmaul, sat demurely on a bent fir tree picking at his splintered long nails and his gray teeth. Nearby a bag lady shivered and rubbed her hands in the evening breeze. She opened up her dusty plaid coat and readjusted the newspaper insulation in her covering. Looking down at the ground, she walked up to the bent tree and noticed some old newspapers lying under branches. She bent over and stuffed the newspapers under the front of her coat. Her hat fell off and she picked it up. As she rose, she sniffed the air to a strong decay. The vampire walked around the bent limb and approached the woman and cocked his head. He grabbed her by the shoulders and lifted her to her feet. The women screamed, fainted, and her head plopped to one side. He went in for the bite languishing as he loudly sucked and drank.

At night, in the park, another bag woman shuffled along with an empty plastic bag. Under a pine tree, the woman in a man's long trench coat saw large pinecones on the ground. Happily, she bent over and collected the cones. *What was that flapping noise?*

Leaning against the tree, a male vampire, Andrain, fluffed his blonde spiky hair. He turned towards the woman and bared his fangs.

The woman looked up and saw the vampire. "Who are you?"

"You're my night cap," he hissed.

The woman screamed, fainted onto the ground, and her head plopped to one side. On bended knee, he went in for the bite. Afterwards, the woman lay on the ground crumpled but still alive. Another vampire, the dark-skinned Peels, approached, turned her to her other neck side and he went in for the bite. His sucking lasted only for a short frustrating moment. Her body lay white-skinned and lifeless. At her age, this death was a cure, not a curse.

The full moon hid with clouds to darken the park path. A scruffy man shuffled along. Tall, thin, unshaven, unwashed. He stopped at a wooden bench near some maple trees. He pulled some rags from his pockets. He put the rags on the bench in one corner as a pillow. He lay down on the bench with his head on the seat facing outward. He swatted mosquitoes from his face. A woman dressed in a long black transparent cloak sat beside him. With long chipped red nails, she stroked his face.

He smiled then opened his eyes. "I like this dream," he whispered through lost teeth.

He turned towards the woman, and she bared her fangs. The man looked up wide-eyed and saw the female vampire, Ineda Bite.

"Now my nightmare." The man screamed and struggled. She went in for the bite. But the taste wasn't there – years of tobacco smoke had thinned the blood.

Near a stand of autumn-brown-leafed oak trees, a bag lady shivered and rubbed her hands. She huddled herself into a crouch position. Her stringy gray hair covered her eyes and lack of teeth. Looking down at the ground, she walked along near a fir tree and noticed some pine needles on the ground. She picked up the pine needles and rubbed them between her hands. She closed her eyes as she smelled her hands of the pungent fir and the crushed needles. She lifted up each armpit at a time, sniffed, and then rubbed each smeared hand to her opposite armpit. She bent over again and picked up some more pine needles and saw a male vampire, Peels, sniffing her. He was confused by this new scent overwhelming her hot blood odor.

"Do I know you?" she peered with crusty eyes. Her eyes widened when she saw his fangs. The woman screamed, dropped the needles from her hands and pushed him away. Struggling with the screaming woman, he leaned in for the bite. His fangs were long and bent causing him difficulty in his attack and more bleeding-out of the victim than sucking in.

At another part of the large park that night, a shabby woman shuffled along with a bag. The coat she had dumpster-dove from a better part of town was camel cashmere but now worn at the collar, elbows, cuffs, and buttons. She stopped at a bench near some trees. She pulled some newspapers from a bag. She put the newspapers on the bench in one corner. She lay down on the bench with her head on the pew facing outward. The sound of wings flapping. The male vampire, Andrain, approached the seat and walked around the sleeping woman. He stroked her face with soft muscular but cold hands.

"Andrew, give me a kiss." She gave a dreamy smile then opened her eyes. She turned towards the vampire, and he bared his pointed but chipped fangs.

"No kiss. A bite and suck." He laughed.

The woman looked up wide-eyed and saw the male vampire. "Andrew – I want Andrew." The woman screamed and struggled. She was no match for the undead. He went in for the bite, but the bite was not sharp, smooth, and fatal – the woman suffered greatly in her thrashing and wailing. She kept calling out for Andrew until her dying breath.

Not far away in the same unpatrolled park, a bag woman shuffled along with an empty tattered plastic bag. Following a path to under a pine tree, the woman saw a trail of cigarette butts on the ground. Happily, she bent over and collected the butts into her bag and pockets. Leaning against the tree, the male vampire, Emmanmaul, fluffed his long curly ebony hair. He turned his red glowing eyes towards the woman and bared his fangs. The woman looked up and saw the vampire.

"Don't I know your mother?" she squinted. His breath was swampy.

The woman screamed, tried to run but her foot got caught on an exposed tree root. The tree shook and disturbed the birds roosting. The vampire pounced on her, but he had to twist her side to side and pull away the numerous ratty scarves and neck clothes to seek an exposed neck to arrange his attack. Her neck folds were flabby and rubbery – like going through chewed, pink, bubble gum.

Two female vampires, Ineda and Scarlett, sat demurely on either side of a bent tree picking at their long nails and hair. Ineda's hair was long, blonde, and unruly, while Scarlett's was shoulder-length, mahogany-red, and wavy. Sitting among the trees, bits of twigs, leaves and fir needles were littered in their hair.

Nearby, a jumble-fashionista dressed woman with a green, cloth, thread-bare bag approached. Looking down at the ground, she walked up to the bent tree and noticed some colorful leaves lying under the branches. "Oh, pretty." She bent over and stuffed the leaves into the bag while admiring each one. Yellow, orange, brown, and mottled green with a musky-sweet smell.

The female vampires walked around the deformed tree and approached the woman from both sides. Both vampires grabbed her by the shoulders.

The woman looked at their wrinkled faces and dirty chipped fangs. "You're not pretty," she started to back away. The woman screamed, fainted, and her head dropped to one side.

One went in for the bite, while the other, Scarlett, stood annoyed. "Hey, I'm standing right here. Leave some for me!" Finished, the first vampire pushed the woman's head to the other side and the other attacked. Not much left but for a snack.

A bag man shuffled along with an empty, mesh, potato bag, kicking at the fir needles on the ground. With his fingers poking out his ripped gloves, he looked under bare branches of trees. Following a path to under a pine tree, the man saw a trail of beer bottles on the ground. Happily, he bent over and collected the bottles into his bag. "Hey, enough for a few fags."

Leaning against the fir tree, a female vampire, Scarlett, fluffed her wavy red hair. She turned towards the man and bared her yellow fangs. The man looked up and saw the vampire. His eyesight wasn't the best especially in this dark park. "Ethel, is that you?"

Then the smell wafted over him – squashed worms, decaying leaves, rotted flesh. The man gagged, fell onto the ground, and his head plopped to one side to retch. On bended knee, the female vampire with her long-twisted nails parted his greasy hair to secure the throbbing spot for her fangs.

A long dark shadow followed under the full moon. A tarty young woman walked along the leaf-lost trees with a leather, couturier bag swung over her shoulder. She stopped at a bench near some trees. She pulled out a book and a flashlight from her bag. She sat seductively; her skirt pulled up to her waist exposing her frilly black undies and read her book with the flashlight. She looked at the glow of her stylish, diamond-encrusted watch, and then looked around. Tiny fireflies skittered around her.

She went back to reading her book. She looked at her watch, and then she glanced around again. A man in a ragged black cape shielding his face approached her. She turned to him and smiled with full red lips. "Zoron, stop playing games."

The man lowered the cape from his face, and he bared his fangs as he sat beside her. His voice was deep and whispery, "No, my name is Zaroon."

The woman beheld wide-eyed the male, ebony vampire, Peels. He grasped her wrists as he belly-laughed as she struggled. Her long red nails couldn't scratch his eyes or anywhere else. He even knew enough to place his black cracked boots on her stiletto heels. He went in for the chew.

Two men walked briskly along a path in the moon-lit park. One looked at his watch. The first man staggering with a limp said, "The girls will freak out that we're late."

Flipping his stringy black hair back, the second man with a stubbled chin said, "Let's take a shortcut off the lighted path." Something flew above their heads.

Two female vampires stood near some bushes and watched the men amble by. Scarlett Le Coeur hissed, "I'm hungry. Dinner just walked by."

Ineda Bite chortled, "I'm thirsty. I'll take the tall one. I need a long drink."

The two men stopped when they saw the dark figures in their path. But when the smell hit them -- *coppery, crusty, and creepy, – they had hesitated a moment too long*. The night sounds were of their suffering.

Bats winged noiselessly in the still night air. A humped-back bag lady shuffled along with an empty, faux-leather bag not looking up from her quest. Following a path under a pine tree, the woman smelt a trail of cigarette butts on the ground. Happily, she bent over and collected the butts into her bag and pockets. Some were stubs, some were broken, and some had lipstick stains.

Leaning against the tree, the male vampire, Emanmaul, puckered his thin lifeless lips. He turned towards the woman and bared his fangs. The woman squinted at the figure. Her eyesight wasn't the best. When he came towards her, she slurred, "These butts are mine. Have you got a light?"

His fangs reflected the moon just unveiled from a cloud. As he moved forward, she thought he was offering her a light, so she took a butt out of her pocket and put it in her toothless mouth. The butt dropped when his fangs pierced the wrinkled skin of her neck. Her screams awoke the resting birds that flew out of the tree in a whoosh.

Chapter 8 - WAREHOUSE ATTACKS

Now with Dr. Drek Vam Dent setting up shop at the industrial warehouse, local vampires hunted here for their blood feasts – many before their dental visit, some even after.

The full moon's craggy surface reflected like a tarnished mirror. Two homeless bag ladies walked along the wall of the building in the warehouse complex.

A newspaper lay tucked under a large garbage bin. A male, Andrain, and a female vampire Ineda, watched the two.

The two women bent over and struggled with each other to get at the newspaper. The wind had picked up thrashing their hair around their faces. "That's mine," said the first woman.

"You got the last paper," said the second with a thinner frayed coat.

The successful one opened her threadbare cotton coat and readjusted the newspaper insulation in her coat. The other one lay on her back with her coat's buttons ripped in the tumble. The air smelled of refuse, rotting flesh, and feces. A rat raced along the wall.

With the two women bent over the ground, the two vampires moved in. The tall, male vampire grabbed the first unsuccessful woman by her skinny shoulders and lifted her to her feet.

The woman screamed wide-eyed and extended lips showing missing teeth. He went in for the bite with loud sucking and slurping.

In the confusion, the female vampire, rakish with extended long, pointed, cracked nails, attacked the newspaper woman twisting her side to side until her dizziness subdued her screams for a neck pierce.

Just around the corner, two hobo men shuffled along looking at the ground. The first man saw a trail of cigarette butts on the ground leading around the garbage bin. Happily, he bent over and collected the butts into his half-ripped pockets of the scruffy brown leather coat.

Behind the bent garbage bin, a mother vampire with her teenage vampire son pointed to the two men. "They may be old, but their blood could be thick – don't suck too fast."

The other man alternated picking up the butts. His coat pockets had holes and the butts made a new trail behind him.

At a larger pile of butts, the two men bent over and greedily scooped them into their pockets. One grubby grabbed a bigger butt, stuck it in his mouth, and then searched in his pants for a lighter.

The first man turned towards the woman vampire and screamed as she bared her long stained fangs.

The other vagrant peered up and perceived the teenage vampire in a tattered black cape. He shrieked then struggled to get up off the ground. On bended knee, the teenage vampire plopped his head to one side, bared his half-formed fangs and plunged in for the bite. The buzz of the outdoor overhead exhaust fan obliterated any human cries.

At a 24-hour recycling business in the warehouse complex, two men exited the back door into the alley. From their jacket inner pockets, they each pulled out a cigarette package. Moths flickered above their heads in the outside light. Two female vampires, Ineda, and Scarlett watched the two. Their wrinkled liver-spotted hands twitched in anticipation.

The older man reached into his industrial pant pocket, pulled out his lighter and lit his cigarette then put his lighter back into his pocket.

The younger man searched his pockets in his stained jeans. "Gimme your light."

The older man reached into his pant pocket, pulled out his lighter again and went to light the younger man's cigarette but dropped the lighter on the ground.

With the older man on the ground struggling in the dark to find the lighter, the two female vampires moved in. Ineda Bite grabbed the first man on the ground by the shoulders and lifted him to his feet. His face mirrored confusion then his mouth opened in a silent scream. Ineda gave him a fanged wink as she ventured in for his neck.

In the confusion, Scarlett Le Coeur purred, "I like my men young."

The man panted and took to run but she grabbed him by the back of his red flannel shirt and bared her crooked fangs. Afterwards, their drained bodies blocked the opening of the door.

At the road entrance to the west-end warehouse complex, two tarty ladies walked along the wall of the building. No car or truck lights drove by. They stopped beside a large, stained garbage bin. An old male and a young female vampire watched the two.

The first woman slurred, "Pretty slow night." Her intake of liquor and drugs were making her wobbly.

Pulling up her elastic-top, ripped, fishnet stockings, the second woman sighed. "I could go for some real action!" She was more coherent but without her glasses, her depth perception was limited. Something bumped against her leg.

The two women bent over and rearranged their clothes. A big gust of wind lifted their short skirts to show their sparkly thongs.

The two vampires swept in. The wrinkled and bent-over vampire grabbed the first woman by her scrawny shoulders. Her right fist connected with his stubbled chin. He roared with laughter as he pushed her to the ground.

A newly-made, blonde vampire already had her cavernous mouth open with jagged fangs ready for maximum penetration onto the other woman. Echoing sounds of sucking, gulping, slurping.

The eastern end of the warehouse complex had a few small manufacturing companies that had a night shift. A young man and woman stood near the overhead doors. They moved closer against the scraped door. The loud motors inside vibrated the door. Standing in the stairwell, two female vampires, Ineda, and Scarlett, watched the two lovers.

The young woman leaned against the wall seductively. "What did you want to talk to me about?" Her tight red cotton top exposing ripe cleavage.

The young man leaned towards her and touched her curled black hair, then her flushed cheek. "Actions speak louder than words." He moved in for a kiss.

The first female vampire, Ineda Bite, grabbed the man by the back of his shoulders. The man screamed, but his fists flew up as he swung around. She batted his fists down as she grasped his head, twisted it to the side and bit.

In the mayhem, the second female vampire seized the whimpering young woman's wrist, pierced the delicate white flesh, and started to suck. When the female victim was drained, she dropped like a ragdoll onto the concrete platform. Her lover was thrown at her in a compromising position.

Two destitute ladies walked along the wall of the warehouse building. Two beer bottles lay tucked under a large graffiti-covered garbage bin. Two male vampires watched the two.

The two street people saw the bottles and ran toward the bin. They had been lucky here before. The two women bent over and struggled with each other to get at the beer bottles. "It's my turn for the refunds. You had it last time," the first with her ragged, fingerless, gloved hands in fists.

"Over my dead body," the second who whipped a shredded, wool, striped scarf to the back.

With the two women wrastling on the ground, the two vampires moved in. Blonde Andrain chuckled, "Ladies, ladies. Your living days are over."

Bowling-ball-bald Peels roared as he grabbed one of the bag ladies and pulled her behind the large garbage bin. Andrain grinned as he watched the second woman try to scramble away on the ground. "The easiest catch of the day."

A beat-up rusty car pulled up to the warehouse alley. Two female vampires, Ineda, and Scarlett watched the car with two young women inside. The first blonde woman replied, "Are you sure this is the address?"

The second redhead woman looked around. "My boyfriend said behind this building. It's open 24-hours so you can job apply anytime."

The two women looked at the alley door with its broken overhead light. The two female vampires moved in. Grey moths were camouflaged against the concrete walls.

The blonde looked around, "It's dark and creepy here. I don't see a buzzer. I'll go and pound on the door."

The redhead sighed and shut off the engine. Opening the car door, the first woman started to get out of the car when Ineda pulled her out of the car by her straight long blonde hair. The woman's arms flayed to break away. Her grunts and groans crested to an animal whine.

The second woman screamed when Scarlett opened the car door and leaned in for the bite. The punching, spitting, and scratching were no deterrent. The two vampires got a different taste that night.

Two other bag ladies walked along the wall of the concrete-block warehouse building. They looked along the ground to pick up rags. A large garbage bin had a pile of rags near a truck wheel. Two female vampires watched the two.

The two bag women saw the rags and ran toward them. They bent on the ground and struggled with each other to get at the rags. "My coat's thinner than yours," the second one shivered.

"My boots aren't lined like yours and I have no socks," complained the first bag lady.

With the two women struggling, the two vampires moved in. They grabbed the two bag ladies and pulled them behind the large garbage bin in the corner. A raccoon silently slipped inside the bin.

Ineda Bite's long twisted fangs pushed through the dirty neck scarf to get a firm grip. Scarlett La Coeur grabbed the other woman's wrist for an easy bite. With her other hand, she smothered the woman's screams.

A young man and woman walked along the wall of the southern warehouse building. The scream of an owl broke the silence. Two female vampires watched the two from behind a large recycling bin.

The humans walked towards a recessed door. The young man felt cold, "We can take a shortcut through the building." He buttoned up his jean jacket against the night air.

The young man pulled at the closed door. The young woman realizing the time, "We're going to be late now." Her legs were bare under her full skirt.

The young man sniffed, "What is that smell?" Dark, dank, disgusting.

The two vampires moved in. One female vampire grabbed the man by the shoulders. The man screamed, fainted, and his head flopped. Ineda Bite bared her fangs, but the man revived and struggled. She dodged his fists but struck her own blow on his forehead.

In the confusion, the other female vampire, Scarlett La Coeur attacked the screaming young woman. She pulled her behind the large garbage bin which now resounded with sucking and glugging. These two female vampires were getting more than their blood share that night.

Two young men stood along the crumbling concrete wall of the north warehouse building. Two female vampires watched the two from behind a large, parked truck.

The first young man with loud, bubble-gum chewing and popping, "What's with those girls?" He looked at his watch.

The other young man grabbed his wrist and looked at the other man's watch. "We're going to be late for the party." He gave a strangled sigh.

The two female vampires strutted in not showing their fangs.

The first young man eyes widened looking at the black clothed hussies. "Hi, girls."

The second young man dressed in jeans and an open-neck plaid shirt tapped his foot. "I don't remember it being a costume party."

Ineda Bite grabbed the first man by the shoulders. "We're having a private party." Taken aback, the man was first amused, but his eyes and mouth widened when he saw her fangs.

Scarlett Le Coeur lifted the other man's chin, "I like my men young and robust." She twisted his head, but his arms went around her waist. "Oh, you want to dance first." She twisted them around, but his grip was fierce. She head-butted him and his grip loosened. She laid him on the ground and turned his head to expose his neck. This was their last party of the night, and the vampires enjoyed the supper.

It was statuesque Dr. Vam Dent's first night of dentistry, and he already had a vampire patient. Word had flown by whispers, sighs, and fang-felt pain. Vampires had teeth and fangs and sometimes they needed attention – abbesses, swollen gums, a loose fang, to name a few.

An older male vampire, Evo, sat on the sagging couch reading a magazine. His small eyes squinted at the small words on the page. His hands shook as he tried to turn the pages. Three younger male vampires, Andrain, Emmanmaul, and Peels, entered up the stairs. Andrain pointed to the old vampire with a dirty nail. "Hey, hey, hey. One long in the tooth."

The other two vambuddies laughed and pushed the old vampire side to side on the couch. The older male vampire dodged from them and back and forth hissing and extending his ragged long nails. He couldn't hide behind his shabby black cape.

Dressed in a black silk suit, Dr. Vam Dent entered the scene with trembling Dr. Moe Lars and pushed the vambuddies away. They stumbled on the ground, but they jumped right up. From his long thin face, Dr. Vam Dent spit out his words, "Too much cholesterol in your blood, Andrain? Do you have to pick on your elders?" _He was even in trouble in his human days._

Andrain faded-rose lips pulled back from his crooked teeth and fangs. "Hey boys – it's time for another bite. No new victims here but they may be just outside the door." He bared his fangs and hissed.

The ebony vampire, Peels, pointed to the exit door. "Yah, Doctor Dentist. We'll make you some more patients. For both of you." Peels' black finger twitched at Dr. Moe Lars whose face became whiter than his stained lab coat.

The three younger male vampires pushed around the older male vampire then left laughing down the stairs. Dr. Vam Dent took the older male vampire into his cubicle followed by Dr. Moe Lars. "I apologize for their intolerant behavior." *How do you kill the undead?*

The older vampire croaked, "I've cursed them, but they only heard themselves."

Later that night, two female vampires, Scarlett La Coeur, and Ineda Bite, sat on either side of Andrain and fussed over him in the disheveled dental office. These bad vamps weren't leaving. A middle-aged woman vampire with a honeybun-hairstyle and her copper-haired teenage son vampire entered the dental scene up the dusty stairs. Andrain reared his stained fangs. "Hey, hey, hey. One really short in the tooth."

The woman vampire whipped her ragged cape away from her. Little bits of rotted, black silk confettied the floor. "You! You are the cause of this. Now his fangs won't come in properly."

From behind the stained plastic shower curtain screen, Dr. Vam Dent entered the conversation. "You're here again, Andrain? Now, you have to pick on innocent teens?" *He lowers himself to depths that are unthinkable.*

Andrain strained himself up to a powerful tall dark shape. "Hey, vee-girls – it's time for a late-night snack." He wasn't talking about the mice that scurried in the dank warehouse.

Picking at her abscessed yellow fang, Ineda Bite taunted, "Doctor Vampire Dentist. Do you prefer male or female?"

Scarlett Le Coeur still clung to Andrain's arm. "How does Doctor Vam Dent like his bites?" She moved her jaw up and down to expose her corroded fangs.

The three vampires pushed around the vampire woman and strained-mouth teen, then left laughing down the stairs out of the warehouse. Dr. Vam Dent took the teen vampire into his cubicle as the woman vampire sat on the creaky couch wringing her hands. If vampires could cry in empathy to her child, she would.

Dr. Vam Dent had brought his old-world technology to this new place. On each finger of his right hand was a mechanized tool – drill, file, scraper, gouger

– using his own cosmic energy to power. The teen was in good dental hands. Dr. Moe Lars, assisting, eyes bulged at the speed and precision of this strange night dentist and his procedures on his other worldly patients.

They came back later – there was a morbid curiosity about the new vampire dental office. The two female vampires, Scarlett La Coeur, and Ineda Bite, sat on the couch reading magazines with two male vampires, Asian Emmanmaul and African Peels, who sat on the ends fussing with them.

Dr. Moe Lars hesitantly approached the couch. His hands shook and sweat formed on his hairless upper lip. "Which dead – I mean man is next?"

The two vampire men jumped up and sparred. Left and right hooks. Steam hissing out of one nose, smoke out of another's ears. The two females growled at each other because they picked their favorite and glared at the fight gymnastics.

Dr. Vam Dent entered the scene. "The electrolytes seem to be off in here." He waved the edges of his ebony satin cape as he walked around the couch. *They are the curses of my new practice.*

With her nostrils flared, Scarlett Le Coeur hissed and nodded toward the human dentist. "I thought he preferred women.

Dr. Vam Dent's eyes flickered red. The scent of sulphur in the air. "I better take you men next." *They aren't privileged to be called men – more like slugs of the earth.*

As Dr. Vam Dent left with the two men vampires pushing them behind the yellowing shower curtain, Dr. Lars wiped at an imaginary dust speck on his stained overcoat. He tried to ignore the little bugs that scurried on the ground.

The two other female vampires tucked in their fangs and purred and cloyed at him, to draw Dr. Moe Lar's attention. Maybe with one eye he did look but pulled his lips to the side in disgust.

Dr. Lars helped Scarlett Le Coeur up from the couch and took her into his cubicle. As she settled in the frayed webbed folding chair, Dr. Lars turned around and saw her bare her fangs and growl. "Now, now, I'm only doing an examination. Dr. Vam Dent will do any other procedures." Scarlett sighed, gave a big smile, and opened her mouth. Dank foul breath spewed. Dr. Moe Lars leaned back in putrid disgust.

The next night, three female vampires sat on the lumpy couch reading magazines. Two younger male vampires, Emmanmaul and Peels, entered the scene up the stairs. Andrain scanned the room with fangs bared. "Hey, hey, hey. I like this fang candy store."

The two other male vampires fussed over the three female vampires. With his black silk hat on his head, Dr. Vam Dent entered the scene and pushed the male vambuddies away. "This is a professional dentist's office. Leave your carousing to the night air." *The sooner they leave the better.*

With his white-ashen face tipped up, Andrain cocked his arthritic-swollen thumb at the black male vampire. "Hey, Peels. Maybe he needs some help with <u>security</u> for his professional office."

Peels smoothed his bald head. "Yah, Doctor Dentist. Maybe you need to hire <u>us</u> to keep out the riff raff." Peel's white straight teeth outshone his coal black skin.

The three female vampires looked annoyed at each other. One hissed at the men vampires. Andrain grinned. "Not like you three hot bites." His voice was cold like the north wind.

Dr. Vam Dent's eyes glowed red. "Are you brave enough for barter?" *Let us see.*

Taken aback, the male vampires clawed in the air at Dr. Vam Dent, and then they left laughing down the stairs. With a smirk, Dr. Vam Dent took one female vampire into his cubicle. The other two female vampires talked among themselves. One said, "I'm glad Dr. Vam Dent stands up to those vamp bullies."

"Yes," the other said. "Andrain just eggs the others to follow his wicked ways."

After taking care of the day's bloodthirsty patients in the waiting area, Dr. Vam Dent arranged magazines on the chipped table beside the stained couch. Three male vampires entered the scene up the stairs. Tall, dark, and gruesome, Andrain, spoke, "Hey, hey, hey. What kind of dental office is this?"

The other two vambuddies laughed and moved around Dr. Vam Dent. They knocked the magazines askew and pinched the couch's fabric. Dr. Vam Dent's voice was as frigid as his stare. "Andrain, Peels and Emmanmaul? Are you here for pleasure or pain?" *Or is it disruption?*

Andrain slinked around the other two male vampires. "Hey boys – which one of you will be first?"

The other two vambuddies cringed and cowed. Peels voice quavered. "Yah, Doctor Dentist. You don't seem too busy. I may..." Then he backed up, tucked his chin down, closed his eyes, and wrapped his black cape around him.

With a big frosty sigh, Dr. Vam Dent said, "It takes time to build up a clientele in any new territory." *But without clients like you.*

Andrain extended his black cape. "As long as you are only servicing and not biting in my territory."

The three male vampires growled and hissed as they exited.

Dr. Vam Dent exhaled frost. As he moved into his cubicle, he pointed his long thin fingers at the male vampires and then abruptly slammed his outstretched arm against his body. Life was so different in the old country.

The next night, the female vampire, Scarlett Le Coeur, sat between two older vampires giving them the bloodshot eye, fishnet leg, and overflowing cleavage. Bywrong, a large-bicep, milk-chocolate-skinned vampire, bopped with his headphones at the entrance side of the couch.

Dr. Moe Lars walked up the stairs as Dr. Vam Dent approached the male vampire patients. "Dr. Moe

Lars, I have Bywrong policing my new practice and keeping my new <u>human</u> dental associate safe and healthy." *My eyes can't be everywhere.*

The three-seated vampires growled and hissed at Dr. Moe Lars. Scarlett fended off the two older male vampires as she stood up. She cocked her head to Dr. Moe Lars. "The throat candy is now hard to chew."

The female vampire snarled and jeered as she left the office. Drs. Vam Dent and Moe Lars took the male vampire patients into their respective cubicles.

Two different female vampires came into the dreary dental office. They sat on the torn couch reading a magazine between them. They took turns turning the pages. Bywrong still bopped at the entrance side of the couch while assessing their dark assets. Drs. Vam Dent and Moe Lars approached the vampire patients. Dr. Moe Lars turned and said to Dr. Vam Dent, "Dr. Vam Dent, I see you now have even more patients. Now you may need even more security."

From his towering stature, Dr. Vam Dent's eyes were piercing red coals. "Dr. Lars, I have Bywrong, my trusted subject, policing my new practice and new dental associate, you, Dr. Moe Lars." *I hope he will be enough.*

Dr. Vam Dent and Bywrong in a friendly manner roared and whistled at each other. Dr. Moe Lars stepped back holding his breath.

The first older female vampire in a black crepe shift stood up, approached Bywrong and stroked his bulging bicep. "I like my security dark and gruesome."

The younger female vampire howled and spat as she left. With his eyebrows raised, Dr. Vam Dent took the lily-white hand of the older woman vampire patient as he led her into a cubicle. Older female vampires had both teeth and fang problems – work that Dr. Vam Dent had done many times in the old country. These new country clients' the problems were textbook.

The blonde woman vampire, Ineda Bite, scrunched beside a googling male vampire giving him an exposure of a finely curved thigh and overabundance of wart-covered cleavage.

Andrain walked up the stairs as Dr. Vam Dent approached the vampire patients. Andrain eyed the two dead and dreary. "Dr. Vam Dent, I see you have even more patients."

Andrain frowned with his lower lip twisted. "Dr. Vam Dent don't worry about your new practice. It may not last long." His hands grabbed the ends of his cape and spun around.

Dr. Vam Dent and Andrain growled and hissed at each other. Long dirty talons ripped the air between them. *Andrain is just a child in my lifespan but still a bother.*

Ineda Bite fended off the other male vampire as she stood up adjusting her overflowing cleavage. "Andrain, let's go someplace darker and more intimate." She sidled up to Andrain's neck and nuzzled it. She grabbed his arm extending her long red bejeweled nails.

The two vampires snarled and jeered as they left. Dr. Vam Dent took the male vampire patient into a cubicle. Another patient with worn down fangs – the bite was definitely off.

Later that night, two women vampires, Scarlett La Coeur, and Ineda Bite, slouched on the couch while another two female vampires stood and talked. The warehouse door creaked open. All eyes turned. Andrain walked up the stairs as Dr. Vam Dent approached the patients. Andrain shook his head with his blond straight-chopped hair falling into eyes. "Dr. Vam Dent, I see you have even more patients. I like the quality." Andrain winked at the vamp girls. He puffed out his naked ripped abs. One vamp girl's lips smacked while another wide-eyed and drooled.

Dr. Vam Dent's black satin cape flicked back and forth as he looked at the patients. "Andrain, and you were worried about my new practice. It didn't take long for new patients." *My reputation is stellar – I have no competition.*

Andrain tapped on his chin then his eyebrows scrunched into a long line. "Take, take. Girls, let's go someplace darker and more intimate." The fine blonde hairs on his chest stood up as in command seducing the vamp girls.

The two standing female vampires howled and jeered as they left with Andrain. Dr. Vam Dent pulled up the arm of one of the female vampire patients from the couch and led her into a cubicle.

A woman vampire sat between two googling men vampires giving them a view of tats and piercings. Andrain walked up the stairs as Dr. Vam Dent approached the patients then turned to Andrain. "Andrain, your voyeur time is over. I need to examine your fangs in my cubicle <u>now</u>." *We'll see how brave he is.*

Andrain's eyes opened as wide as his mouth. "Dr. Vam Dent, you, you can't make me a patient."

Dr. Vam Dent gave a deep throaty chuckle. "You don't have to worry about the difference between pleasure and pain." *I'll make sure you have a lot of pain.*

Dr. Van Dent unfurled his hand. Andrain saw the instruments on Dr. Vam Dent's fingers as extensions – the whirring drill, the curved pick, the pointed pincers, and extraction forceps. Andrain almost fell back. He cried a high piercing shrill at the other vampires as they cowered on the thin-bare couch.

The female vampire fended off the other vampires as she sat up. "Andrain, you can take my place next."

Andrain whimpered as he left, his ragged black cape dragging in the stairwell's dust and grime.

Dr. Vam Dent took one of the men vampire patients into a cubicle and left the female vampire to fuss on the other frightened male vampire. As expected.

Two female vampires, Scarlett La Coeur, and Ineda Bite, sat on the couch preening. Bywrong bopped to his inner-ear techno music at the entrance side to the warehouse door of the couch.

Dr. Vam Dent approached the new vampire patient, Jamie Lee, in long dread locks. She cooed and licked her lips as she pointed to Bywrong. "Dr. Vam Dent, you need real security; not some distracted slug."

Dr. Vam Dent's nostrils flared as his eyes widened. "Bywrong is all eyes and ears and fangs." *You just tried the thing wrong.*

The two female vampires and Bywrong growled and hissed at each other with a black skunk smoke surrounding them. Two male vampires, Emmanmaul and Peels, walked up the stairs and observed the scene.

The first skeleton-thin male vampire, Emmanmaul, beckoned with a skinless finger. "Girls, this can get dark and gruesome. Let's get come cold, grave air."

Bywrong bared his long sharp fangs and clawed his hands at them as the four left. Peeking from behind the ragged plastic curtain, Dr. Vam Dent observed the scene, then went into his cubicle with Jamie Lee.

It was winter and the sun didn't rise until late in the morning. The warehouse door opened and a courier man in a brown uniform entered. He walked up the stairs slowly looking around suspiciously. Two white-bone faced female vampires flanked a grave-dead looking male vampire preening him. Dr. Vam Dent approached the stairs. His face ashen, the courier man stuttered, "I had a hard time finding this place."

Dr. Vam Dent glowed in intensity. "Our sign is being made next door. Here is the parcel." *The longer dark makes human interaction unavoidable.*

The courier man chewed on his words. "Since you haven't been in business for six months, it must be pre-paid, but…but I'll get it next time."

As he ran out the door, another courier man, this one in a green short-sleeved logoed shirt and green shorts, sauntered in. "That's good I saw the last guy coming out, I couldn't find the place."

Dr. Vam Dent's lips curled in a sneer. "I'll go next door in a minute and find out what's taking them so long with the sign." *The anonymity suits me best.*

The second courier man looked around. His lower lip trembled. His mouth turned chalk white. "This parcel is COD, please, but I see you are busy. I don't mind paying this time."

He leaped out the door. On the receptionist's desk, Dr. Vam Dent opened a heavily carved wooden box containing jewels, shrugged and took the male vampire into his cubicle. Dr. Moe Lars had left early from his night shift so there were no humans to deal with the outside business distractions.

The warehouse door creaked opened and an older woman vampire, Ethel, with a basket entered. Her black dress was ragged, ripped, and stained. She walked up the stairs and looked around suspiciously. A trio of older women vampires hunched on the couch looking at magazines. Ethel said, "I don't feel so bad now, I know someone."

She crouched on the arm of the couch beside one of the women vampires. The first vampire lady, Sophia, cooed, "Ethel, I haven't seen you in a bat's age."

Dr. Vam Dent took one of the old vampire ladies, Gladys, into his cubicle. The last vampire lady, Martha, chimed, "Don't hurry Doctor. We have a lot of catching up to do."

Sophia, her long grey hair in natural ringlets, peered over. "What have you got in your basket there?"

Ethel showed a basket with a dried severed hand, a crusty eyeball, a skinless leg bone, a bloody ear, and some yellow loose teeth.

The warehouse door opened, and warehouse owner, Hans Weiner, entered. He walked up the stairs and looked around suspiciously at the three old vampire women on the couch and the basket. "This isn't a proper dental office, it's a ..."

The vampire lady, Sophia, pulled a hairy severed leg out of a velvet matted bag with a worn wooden handle. Before speaking anymore, Hans put his hand to his mouth, gagged, and ran out.

The night wind whipped the clouds on a race among the stars. A hearse pulled up to the industrial door where the 24-hour dental office sported its new sign. The male vampire driver exited and opened the door for an older distinguished male vampire to get out.

Two beautiful women vampires in their flowing black lace gowns hunched on the couch, talked among themselves, and looked at the dental magazines. The older male vampire, Count Vam Dent, walked up the stairs and looked around; his face soured, his lips pulled back. His black-pupiled eyes grew red in disgust as his eye wrinkles formed and his mouth sneered with fangs showing.

As Dr. Vam Dent approached the vampire patients, one female vampire stood up. They both turned and looked at the new visitor.

Count Vam Dent spit out, "Drek Vam Dent, what is this now? You have traded your vampire nobility and heritage for the service to other vampires?"

The other vampires nodded and smiled at Dr. Vam Dent. They didn't dare look at the older vampire.

Dr. Vam Dent spoke slowly, "Count Vam Dent, my fellow vampires. I am honored to be of service to them, Father." *Oh, no. Just as I am starting my new practice.*

Dr. Vam Dent took one of the female vampire patients into a cubicle. Up the stairs came Andrain and Peels. Andrain spoke complaisant but smug. "Count Vam Dent, we are honored for your presence in our region. Are you here to visit your son, Dr. Drek Vam Dent?"

With a flip of his satin black cape, Count Vam Dent sat on the couch. "Visit wouldn't be a word I'd use."

Standing over her, the other two male vampires pushed around the other female vampire on the couch and growled and hissed at her to the disgust of Count Vam Dent. "You're not acting your century ages."

Dr. Vam Dent came back into the waiting room with the first female vampire. She went over to the box and deposited some jewels. As Dr. Vam Dent approached the second female vampire on the couch, Count Vam Dent stood up with a great puff of air to make his cape unfurled. They all turned and looked at the out-of-place visitor.

Count Vam Dent scolded, "Dr. Vam Dent, son, I had no time to wait. I need to give you this amulet against the Shadow Attackers."

From his pocket in a box, Count Vam Dent pulled out an old gold medallion on a red bedraggled velvet ribbon. The treasure was dark with a large pulsating ruby in the center. A low hum came from the gem.

Dr. Vam Dent staggered back. "Count Vam Dent, Father. I am honored that I may have this talisman now." Dr. Vam Dent took the medallion in his hand and the red stone beat in double time. *At last, he acknowledges me as his rightful son.*

Up the warehouse stairs came Andrain and Peels. Andrain looked at the pair with fangs bared. "Count Vam Dent, old man. We control this region now as Shadow Attackers."

The two male vampires lunged at the other two men. Dr. Vam Dent flashed the medallion as it screamed at them. They left, hissing and growling. *Now I have stronger power against them.*

The two women vampires on the couch whispered and nodded among themselves. Count Vam Dent put his arm around Dr. Drek Vam Dent, and they entered his cubicle.

Two men and three women vampires lounged on the couch and its arms and talked among themselves. As Dr. Vam Dent approached the patients, one female vampire stood up. "Dr. Vam Dent, your excellent dental work is well known in the region. I am honored for you to take me on as a patient."

The other vampires nodded and smiled at Dr. Vam Dent. The second female vampire continued, "I hope some of my family jewels can be but meager payment for your excellent services."

The standing female vampire took the wooden jewel box off the table and put in sparkling diamonds, red rubies, faceted emeralds, and soft pink pearls from her handbag. The others also put priceless gems into the box.

Dr. Vam Dent would have blushed if he had any blood in his cheeks. "My fellow vampires. You do me the honor of being of service to you." He bowed low from his waist. His tall black hat never faltered. *This is why he left the old country to service the new vampires.*

Dr. Vam Dent escorted one of the female vampire patients like the high nobility she was from the faded couch into a cubicle. The other vampires nodded, smiled, and talked among themselves.

That night, no unusual shadows followed as the warehouse door opened and Miss Connie and Aunty

Mae Lars entered. They walked up the stairs looking around suspiciously. Dr. Vam Dent approached them. Aunty Mae Lars spoke, "The office looks so different, almost beautiful. I could work here at night."

Dr. Vam Dent pointed out, "Our new sign '24 Hour Dental Clinic, Open to Both Teeth and Fangs, No Appointment Necessary' has being made next door. I hope to get more patients soon."

He approached Miss Connie and held her hand. She blushed and turned her head. Dr. Vam Dent smiled, "I don't think Dr. Moe Lars will mind if I change you to my patient." She dropped Dr. Vam Dent's hand and sat down on the couch with Aunty Mae Lars perched on the couch's arm.

Andrain, Peels and Emmanmaul walked up the stairs. Andrain ranted, "Patients, patients. How will your associate dentists like you stealing their patients?"

Dr. Vam Dent hissed. "Miss Connie is more than a patient. She is special." *Yes, to me.*

Andrain chuckled. "Special in our world can only mean one thing."

The three male vampires lunged forward to attack Miss Connie on the couch. Dr. Vam Dent pulled the red jeweled medallion that his Count father had given him from under his jacket and flashed it towards them. They ran out, screaming and hissing.

Dr. Vam Dent stepped back. "Things have progressed faster than I expected." *Much too fast.*

He took Aunty Mae Lars into his cubicle. "If you are serious about working for me, there will need to be a few changes."

Aunty Mae Lars smiled and nodded. Dr. Vam Dent pulled his cape over Aunty Mae Lars. His bite on her was not sensual or threatening but speedy and efficient.

Aunty Mae Lars' reaction was not pleasure, not pain, but knowledge of eternal life. "I feel refreshed, I feel…"

Dr. Vam Dent grinned, "Undead. Now, your new name will be Rozdent. A new member of my family." *Yes, I'll grow my new family here.*

Rozdent was transformed from a frumpy female to a curvaceous vamp with piercing eyes wrapped in calf-length black tulle with a black silk liner.

That evening, the warehouse door opened and Dr. Pierce Able entered. He walked up the stairs and looked around suspiciously.

A male vampire with a bag of blood hanging from his mouth seemed to be asleep. On the table, Dr. Pierce Able opened an old carved wooden small casket-container filled with jewels, gold, silver, platinum coins, and artifacts. His mind and fingers started figuring.

Dr. Vam Dent approached him with Miss Connie snickering. Dr. Pierce Able said, "The office looks so different, but so dark. I couldn't work here." Dr. Able stood ridged with his hands on his hips. He tapped his foot nervously.

Dr. Vam Dent said, "Good evening, Dr. Pierce Able. No worry. Your partner, Dr. Moe Lars, will help me as my practice swells." *Yes, I could never trust you.*

Andrain, Peels, and Emmanmaul walked up the stairs hissing and growling. Dr. Vam Dent said, "Miss Connie, I'll walk you home after this next patient."

Dr. Pierce Able leered at Connie, the roundness of her form in a V-neck top. "I'll escort Miss Connie if you want to deal with these three gentlemen."

Miss Connie left with Dr. Pierce Able as the male vampires hissed, growled, and lunged at each other. They didn't dare do that to Dr. Vam Dent.

Dr. Vam Dent put on a devious smile, "Miss Connie, I need to visit you tonight." His eyes glowed red at the three male vampires, his fangs extended. *Yes, it has to be tonight.*

Dr. Moe Lars had been listening in the back and watching, but he didn't dare enter.

Later that night, Dr. Moe Lars walked up the stairs to the front door of Connie's apartment house. He knocked at the door. He waited then knocked again.

In her attic apartment, Connie put on the robe to her white negligee set. She sat on her bed putting rose-scented cream on her hands, face, neck, and cleavage. A knock at the attic door startled her.

Hesitantly, she said, "Who is it?" She moved toward the door and opened it.

She didn't need to ask. "Dr. Vam Drek -- it is very late."

Drek took her by the shoulders and gently pushed her onto the bed. He ran his cool long finger along her neck. She shivered and lifted her head to him. "I haven't done this before."

Drek's eyes burned red. "I have waited a long time." *Yes, for the right virgin woman.*

He took off her robe. He laid her on the bed. He placed his face into her neck. Connie moaned. He pulled his cloak to cover them both.

Dr. Moe Lars walked up the stairs to the second level. He closed the door behind him then walked up the stairs to the attic. In the gloomy light on the walls, he didn't notice the cough and sneezy slime and muddied fingerprints.

On the attic landing his hand gripped the splintered railing. He hesitated as he heard a loud orgasmic moan and a creak of a mattress spring.

He pounded one fist into the other palm. With a grimace, he shrugged and went back down the stairs.

A few nights later, a hearse pulled up to the door, the male vampire driver exited and opened the door for an older male vampire to get out. Inside the warehouse dental office, two older women vampires sat on the couch, talked among themselves, and looked at the magazines.

Count Vam Dent walked up the stairs and looked around disgustingly. As Dr. Vam Dent approached the patients, they both turned and looked at the new visitor.

Count Vam Dent spoke, "Dr. Vam Dent, son, I see you are servicing your mother and aunt."

Dr. Vam Dent took a second long look at the women. "Countess Vam Dent, Duchess Vam Dent, I'm sorry but I didn't see you both come in." *My thoughts are too elsewhere.*

Her bejeweled tiara caught the low light. Countess Vam Dent strained to lean forward on the worn couch. "Word has spread far and wide of your excellent work, my son." She gave a wink and wide smile to him. Duchess Van Dent nodded. She fingered the large deep-green emeralds around her neck.

Up the stairs came Andrain. He slinked against the wall observing the scene. Duchess Vam Dent used her cane to help herself straighten up on the lumpy couch. "Just in time. My old fangs."

Count Vam Dent sat between the two women vampires, and they talked and nodded among themselves as Dr. Vam Dent stood beaming.

Dr. Vam Dent turned his head and noticed Andrain watching the scene. With a flip of his leathery black cape and a blast of sewage-smelling air, Andrain left.

The night was ink dark early when the creaky warehouse door opened, and Hans Weiner entered. He didn't like to go to this part of town at night. He didn't like to go to this dental business. He walked up the stairs looking around suspiciously. Three female vampires sat on the couch reading magazines, looked up, sniffed, and bared their teeth. Andrain and Peels walked up the stairs hissing and growling behind him.

Hans Weiner's throat clenched, and his hands shook. His German accent stronger than ever. "I know one of the dentists will be here any minute."

The vampires encircled Hans Weiner. Andrain poked at his round belly. "Peels, we may not have to feed for a week after this one."

Hans Weiner galloped down the stairs with the two male vampires after him. Coming out of his cubicle with Count Vam Dent, Dr. Vam Dent stepped forward to go after the group but was stopped with a firm hand on his shoulder by Count Vam Dent. "You must throw the wolves their morsels."

Dr. Vam Dent stood up straight. "Father, you don't the ways of humans here." *We will have more terror to pay.*

With a pained look in his granite eyes, Dr. Vam Dent turned and went back into his cubicle. Count Vam Dent shrugged and approached the female vampires with a large fang smile.

Two female vampires, Ineda and Scarlett flanked a male vampire fussing over him and fingering his fangs to his extreme discomfort. Dr. Vam Dent stood in his cubicle with an older female vampire with her back turned. They approached the far end of the coach where there was a table and chair.

Dr. Vam Dent moved close, "You can rearrange the office as you like, Rozdent." *I need to give her some crumbs.*

Rozdent gasped. "My first day on the job and I'm treated like nobility."

Andrain walked up the stairs and approached the couch. "Ineda Bite and Scarlett Le Coeur, I told you vamps not to hang around here."

Ineda fluttered her long disease-crusted eyelashes. "I'm fascinated by all the new dead here." She pointed at Rozdent.

Scarlett leaned forward to caress Andrain's leg. "You can't bite all the time; play sometime."

With his blond hair spiked, Andrain grabbed the two female seated vampires and pulled them into a standing position. "Vamps, your fangs are needed elsewhere."

Andrain hissed at the two struggling females then Dr. Vam Dent. Dr. Vam Dent and Rozdent watched the trio leave. Dr. Vam Dent gave out a heavy sigh. "Rozdent, never turn your back on Andrain or his entourage. Even as you are one of us now." *They are always the enemy.*

The next night the warped warehouse door opened and Dr. Pierce Able entered. He walked up the stairs looking around suspiciously. No one was sitting on the couch. No one was sitting at the reception desk. No one was in the dental cubicles. He had checked. On the table, he opened the large crafted wooden box filled with jewels. He scooped the precious gems into his stained white overcoat pocket.

Without a sound of their entrance, Andrain, Peels, Emmanmual, Ineda Bite and Scarlett Le Coeur, walked up the stairs hissing and growling. Caught with his hands full of the valuable stones, Dr. Pierce Able's face dripped with sweat and his hands and voice trembled. "I know Dr. Vam Dent will be here any minute." *Crap! I've been caught.*

The vampires encircled Dr. Pierce Able. Their capes flapped, their talons poised, their fangs exposed. Andrain stood up tall and menacing, his voice stern. "As there is honor and respect among professionals; there is sanctuary among vampires."

Dr. Pierce Able scrunched smaller and clenched his fists to his chest. "Oh, these things in my pockets are just …" *Believe me, believe me!*

Andrain's voice raged like the wind through a tunnel. "Jewels from our fellow vampires past lives and fair payment for Dr. Vam Dent's excellent services."

Dr. Pierce Able clutched his throat with both trembling hands. "I was just collecting this month's rent. Nothing for myself, of course." *Believe me, believe me!*

Andrain lunged forward with his fangs bared. "Vamps, you can have him as dessert. Peels, Emmanmaul and I will have him as main course."

All the vampires attacked Dr. Pierce Able. Biting, piercing, sucking, ripping, clawing, scraping.

Later that night, the warehouse door scraped opened and a female vampire, the former Miss Connie, now Rouge Throat, entered. She walked up the stairs looking around in awe. Her shoulder-length straight blonde hair glowed against her black-fitted, beaded, silk knee-length dress. Her skin was luminous.

On a couch sat two female vampires, two male vampires perched on the couch arms and another male vampire stood beside them talking to each other. They all turned, looked at her and sniffed the air.

The first female vampire cooed, "You're new, sweet blood. Come and sit beside me. Don't mind them."

The second female vampire spoke in a hushed voice. "They wish!"

The standing male vampire strut about, "Just wait till I get my fang fixed." His eyes widened. He gave her a wink and smiled wide with missing teeth.

The left couch vampire laughed, "You're too long in the tooth for any action."

With a flip of his loose wrist, the left couch vampire replied, "With today's fashions, it's hard to tell."

Squeezed with the female vampires on the couch, Rouge Throat had her first eyeful looking apprehensively at all the vampires.

The orange globe sun had just set when a raven-haired woman, leggy with green eyes entered, walked up the stairs looking around with a big bright smile. The trio of Dr. Moe Lars and Dr. Vam Dent and his hefty sidekick, Bywrong, with headphones, stood beside the desk. The woman approached the desk. "I'm so sorry to hear that your aunt – receptionist has left, but goody for me."

Dr. Moe Lars grabbed her hand while leering down her sequenced-trimmed, low-cleavage, top bursting out, "I'm glad you came back to take this position."

With his red dark-hooded eyes, Dr. Vam Dent grabbed her hot other hand with his icy fingers. "Hello, I'm Dr. Moe Lars' new partner, Dr. Drek Vam Dent, and my associate Bywrong." *Mmm, another human hot morsel.*

The woman gripped tighter Dr. Moe Lars' hand but shook off Dr. Vam Dent's death grip. "Oh goody, my name is Wanda Lotta. I can't wait to start helping you both."

The door opened and a man started up the steps. The brown curly-haired man approached the desk with a sheet of typed paper in his hand.

Dr. Moe Lars spoke up. "I'm not busy, I can take you now." He moved towards the young man dressed in navy medical scrubs.

"No, I'm here to apply as a dental hygienist. My name is Teddy Tusk." His wide toothy smile turned upside-down when he saw Dr. Vam Dent and Bywrong.

He gulped as Dr. Lars, Wanda Lotta, Dr. Drek Vam Dent, and Bywrong encircled him.

Dr. Vam Dent spoke up first. "The moon is on the rise; our night clientele will drastically increase."

The woman and man looked at the others suspiciously. Dr. Vam Dent nodded then spoke in his deep voice, "For now, Ms. Lotta, take his resume."

Wanda moved behind the desk and the man stood in front raising his eyebrows at her as her shoulders shrugged in answer.

After Dr. Lars, Dr. Drek Vam Dent and Bywrong moved into a cubicle, Wanda whispered, "I think strange things happen here, and not all dental."

The two continued their whispering with their heads together.

A loud death-toll banging sounding like cannon fire shook the dental office. Dr. Van Dent rushed into the office area and held back Dr. Moe Lars and Bywrong. Wanda and Teddy were huddled under the school desk used in the reception area.

"Don't even dare to go near the door," Dr. Vam Dent's voice shuddered. "I know who it is. It is not welcome, and it means us harm." His red medallion pulsed to fill the room with a blood color…

About the author

Christine J. Whitlock, a Hamilton ON Canada writer, has a Magazine Journalism Cert. from Ryerson U, and Creative Writing and Novel Writing Certs from George Brown College, Toronto.

She has indie-published (32) non-fiction books in cycling, business, and erotica.

Christine wrote/directed/indie-produced (4) horror feature films: SHARP TEETH, VAMPIRE DENTIST, MARINA MONSTER, and DAYS OF THE IGUANAS.

Six horror short stories have been published.

Interested in getting the latest scoop on new and upcoming books written by the author? Email her directly to subscribe: Write Subscribe in the subject heading.

Christine J. Whitlock
C: 905/512-8123
info@cjcpinc.com, www.cjcpinc.com